D1481171

The Genessee Queen

DELACORTE PRESS/NEW YORK

The Genessee Queen

A novel by

WINIFRED MADISON

Published by
Delacorte Press
1 Dag Hammarskjold Plaza
New York, New York 10017

Manufactured in the United States of America

First printing

Designed by Leonard Telesca

Library of Congress Cataloging in Publication Data

Madison, Winifred.
The Genessee Queen.

SUMMARY: When their volatile mother decides to leave
their father, Monica and her sister reluctantly accompany
her to a small island off the coast of Canada.
[1.   Family problems—Fiction.   2.   Mothers and
daughters—Fiction.   3.   Islands—Fiction]   I.   Title.
PZ7.M2652Gc   [Fic]   77–72634

ISBN 0–440–02809–4

For my friends on the Island

"They [women] attach themselves to places; and their fathers—a woman's always proud of her father."

—Virginia Woolf,
Mrs. Dalloway

PROLOGUE

1

A Hasty Departure

At first Monica thinks she is having a nightmare. Her mother is shaking her gently, all the while whispering, "Come, darling. Time to get up. We have to leave."

The bedside clock states that it is ten-oh-five, but it is still night. Monica burrows under the covers, for she wants so much to sleep, but Irina pulls the blankets away.

"Monica, get up *now*! It's almost too late. No time to sleep."

Monica hears the urgency in her mother's voice and sits up with a jerk, wide awake now. It's not a dream after all. Her mother is pulling clothes from her closet and cramming them into a suitcase . . . jeans, shirts, sweaters, a few dresses.

"Mother, what's going on? What on earth are you doing?"

"We're going on a trip. I'll explain later."

"At this time of night? But Daddy's playing a concert, the double concerto with Julie, that cellist . . ."

"That's why we're leaving," Irina interrupts curtly.

"Oh, Mother, that's dumb!" Irina pays no attention, but rummages through the drawers of Monica's bureau.

"Are these all the socks you've got? They're full of holes."

"Mother, I'm not going, I'm simply not going," Monica states, sitting up stubbornly with her arms around her knees as if nothing can possibly move her.

"I'm not asking you, I'm *telling* you. Gabrielle's dressed and waiting downstairs. Now get with it. Hurry!"

"But I can't leave now. Next week is the recital and I'm playing the Beethoven sonata. I've been working on it for months . . ."

As helpless tears begin to sound in her voice, her mother softens, sits beside her, and hugs her. Her voice becomes lower, huskier, and touching as it takes on an indefinite European accent. "Darling, I can't explain everything to you now, but later you will understand. Believe me, nobody loves you more than I do, so trust me. Okay, Monica? And *hurry*!"

Monica is twelve years old and more frightened than she dares to admit. As she dresses, she comforts herself by shrugging off this escapade as one of her mother's little dramas, this one more elaborate than usual. Irina cannot help it; it is her nature to be dramatic. It happened when Monica's father flirted with a certain blonde sculptress in San Francisco, and then there was that South American singer, and now an auburn-haired student cellist; does her mother really think that she, Monica, does not understand? In the past Irina took her daughters to a friend's house or to a motel, only to wait for Josef's call, his apologies and his promises that it would never happen again. Then they made up, embraced each other, laughed and cried noisily, and went home to live together until the next affair.

This time, Monica does not want to go, not at all. Why, then, does she pull on her jeans and jersey and move slowly down the stairs? Why does she linger on the sidewalk and stare at this vaguely Spanish house with its small sign that says in orange letters LA CALIFORNIE, as if she wants to fix it in her mind forever? This house in Berkeley has been home now for two years—the only home she has ever known.

"I'm not going," Monica shouts defiantly. "I won't go. I won't!"

"And you won't have a tantrum either," her mother says, opening the front door of the car. "Get in now and stop this nonsense. We're not going far."

"Then why did you pack all those clothes?"

"Shh, you'll wake Gabrielle," Irina says, but Monica's little sister is hardly asleep. Wide-eyed with apprehension, Gabrielle whispers to Monica in the front seat.

"What's Mommy doing? I don't want to go anywhere."

"Don't worry, Gaby. It will probably be all right. Wouldn't you like to go to sleep?" How easy it is to comfort someone else, but who will assure Monica that everything will be all right?

Content that the trunk of the car is packed, Irina sits in the driver's seat with a long cigarette holder clenched between her teeth. Nobody says a word, but as she drives north toward the highway, Monica fears that this trip may be longer and more serious than the others. Now she cajoles her mother.

"Mama, let's go back, okay? We can still get there before Daddy gets home. Anyway, he doesn't really like Julie; he's just acting. You know. He's only playing."

"That's exactly it. I don't like the games he's playing. He needs to know it. Don't worry, Monica. I left a note and the phone number and chances are we'll be back soon enough."

"How soon?"

"In time for your recital, I'll bet. Now don't worry."

But Monica does worry as the hills of the Bay cities, sparkling with lights, disappear behind them. They are driving north, and on this night it is cold, dark, and unwelcoming.

"Mother, where are we going? I mean, *exactly* where?"

"To Genessee. Don and Mary Canfield are letting us use their cottage. A beautiful place. Remember, Daddy and I visited there last summer when you were at music camp?"

"But Mother! Genessee Island is in *Canada*!" This is a nightmare after all. "It's very, very far."

"But you'll love it," Irina says in a soothing voice, "and chances are we'll be home before the week is out. Wait and see. Your father will never let us go. He can't live without us."

Monica wants to believe this, takes one last look at the Berkeley hills. "I'm coming back anyway," she promises.

Gabrielle sleeps most of the way and Monica dozes off intermittently, but Irina drives steadily north, stopping only for gas and occasional meals at Sambo's or Denny's.

"Order anything you like," she tells the girls, as though this were a holiday, but there is no gaiety and little hunger. Gabrielle whines that she wants to go home.

The April they have left behind with its mild breezes and radiant blooming becomes winter grim and chilly as they near Canada. Again Monica pleads with her mother as they approach the border, for the official leave-taking seems so final, but Irina drives on silently, turning left to drive down a long flat road that is gray in the light of the late afternoon. It leads to a harbor where a large ferry gleaming white in the blue grayness of the day appears to be waiting for them. THE GENESSEE QUEEN is printed on its hull in clear blue letters.

Monica senses genuine panic within her now as Irina drives the car into the belly of the ferry ship and urges her daughters to climb to the deck above. Monica imagines the boat stopping at a tiny, desolate island in the middle of this endless ocean, a tiny dot of land where they will be abandoned forever. She shivers beside her mother on the deck while the seagulls mew and cry as they wheel above them.

"Mother, I'm scared. We'll never get back."

Irina reaches for her daughter's hand and presses it to give her courage. "I know how you feel, darling, but you mustn't be afraid. This ferry is our friend; you know what I mean? It goes to the Island several times every day and it always waits there a little in case you want to go back to the mainland. It will never fail you. You can always go back."

She smiles encouragingly, though her face is white with lack of sleep. The ferry whistle blasts: there is a shouting, a creaking of ropes, and a gust of wind blows harshly.

"Gabrielle and I are going inside the cabin," Irina says. "Want to come with us, Monica?"

"No!" she cries curtly. Her mother has made a monstrous error, and her comforting words do not quiet Monica's fears. Alone and trembling, Monica walks to the front of the ferry as it moves calmly through the cold blue waters of the north.

2

The Escape

Her fears about the Island are unjustified. Instead of a small stony desert, Genessee Island is a large pleasant expanse of farmland, woodlands, pastures, a mountain, several ponds, and a village center with the usual cluster of churches, grocery stores, gas station, restaurant, and several small newish shops. The cottage that bears its name—BITTERSWEET PLACE—in faded old-fashioned letters over the front porch appeals to Monica as being just the sort of place she would love if only her father were there with them.

"It will be all right for a few days," she says. She has no choice now but to share her mother's belief that any moment the telephone will ring or he will have driven north for the dramatic effect of walking through the front door and saying hello casually, as if the trip were nothing at all. And then of course he will take them all home.

The dark upright piano in the living room of the cottage has lost a few keys and obviously has not been tuned for years, yet Monica practices the Beethoven sonata; how fortunate that she has memorized it, and yet she wishes she could look over the music once more. As long as she practices, she believes her father will come. The day before the recital in Berkeley is to take place, she worries and telephones him, but he is not at home and the secretary at the office says he cannot be reached. The day of the recital comes and goes without a word from him. It is then that Monica closes the lid on the piano.

"Well, don't feel bad," Irina comforts her. "There'll be other recitals."

Irina has already found friends on the Island. The day after the scheduled recital a splendid gray-haired woman, an artist who lives alone and has taken on the title of Aunt Kathryn, invites Irina and the girls to go fishing with her. Monica complains of a headache but urges Irina and Gabrielle to go without her. Once they leave, she quickly packs a small canvas bag, takes her savings, and borrows five dollars from her mother's purse—she is careful to leave an I.O.U.—and practically runs down the road for three miles to the ferry slip. She has only enough money to get her to Seattle, she thinks, but once she is there she will call her father and he will come and get her or wire money to her.

"I think he will fly up to get me," she supposes as she stands at the rail of *The Genessee Queen*, gazing over the blue waters and the green islands of the gulf. She pictures his anguished face as he searches for her in the bus station and how he will hold her and insist that she go back to Berkeley with him. After all, he has no reason to be angry with her.

After the ferry lands, Monica inquires about buses to the States, and within a few hours of leaving Genessee has found the bus station in Vancouver and has boarded the bus. Proud of herself for having figured her way, she sits back confidently as the flat landscape flashes by. But she has forgotten the officials at the border. They board the bus and question each passenger.

"Identification, please? Where do you live? How long will you be visiting?" They are cool; they are polite, even kind, but the panic mounts within her. She has no identification, no letter from parent or guardian, nothing. Frightened, she follows the official off the bus, which leaves without her, and she is questioned inside the station. She sits on the edge of a chair and wishes she could grow smaller and smaller like Alice in Wonderland. She would not even mind disappearing, she is so miserable. The police officials are very kind, and one of them brings her a cup of hot chocolate.

"We would like to call your parents," one of them says, "so they can come and get you."

Her voice quivers as she gives them her father's name and telephone number. The officer calls from another office and Monica cannot hear the conversation, but it seems to be a long one. She waits and finally the officer explains what has happened. "Your father says that your mother is in charge of you. He gave us her number, so we called her. She's missed the last ferry, she says, but promises to pick you up tomorrow morning."

"And my father didn't even want to talk to me?" Monica asks.

The officer cannot stand the pain and disbelief in her voice, so he stretches the truth to save her. "Well, he wanted to know if you were all right and then he admitted that he would love to see you, but there could be legal involvements and he thought it would be best if you stayed with your mother."

Monica is silent as she is driven to the Juvenile Hall in Bellingham, Washington, where she spends the night. She is pale, cannot eat dinner or breakfast the next morning, and is too grief-stricken to talk with the other unhappy girls, who are there for different reasons.

Her mother arrives at nine-thirty. Monica is braced for a scolding in her mother's loudest, most abrasive Hungarian voice, which will ring all over Juvenile Hall so that everyone will know what she has done. But she is wrong. Irina, quiet and pale, embraces Monica.

"Come, Monica, let's go home," she says.

Home! So now the Island has become home? "I was so worried that something had happened to you, and I'm so relieved that you are all right. You must never do this again, Monica. It is too much," Irina says as they drive north.

"I didn't mean to worry you or hurt you," Monica answers in a weak voice.

"I know," Irina says. "You wanted to see your father."

"He didn't want me back!" The words explode from Monica and she sobs, her shoulders shaking. "He didn't want me back!" she repeats.

"No, darling, that's not true. He's a stubborn man and he's angry right now, but when he gets over his bad temper and his vanity, you'll see—he'll beg all of us to go back. I think he will come to Genessee to get us; he loved it here, so he won't mind the trip. Trust me, Monica—he will come for us sooner or later."

Irina is so positive that Monica almost believes her. Can it be a matter of faith after all?

"I'll bet you're hungry. Let's stop off at one of these restaurants and you can have some cheese cake. You can have some coffee, too. I know your favorites! And I'll tell you about some wonderful people I met today, two fine men who have a goat farm . . ."

Irina chatters as Monica sips her coffee. She still smarts from the rebuff from her father. It's all Irina's fault, she thinks, and yet her mother tries so hard to comfort her that she has to forgive her at least ninety percent—no, ninety-five percent. But there is still a tiny knot of resentment against her mother; it lodges within her and will not go away.

3
A Decision

In the days that follow, Monica writes to her father, six letters in all, carefully spaced in case he should answer one of them. In the first she forgives him for not having talked to her when she was at the border, but surely he should know that a girl will be just as well off with her father as with her mother. Her other letters are winsome, poetic, nostalgic, loving, and pleading in tone, but they don't work; he doesn't answer.

Instead a letter arrives for Irina, a letter from a legal firm in Berkeley. Her face becomes white as she reads it and she complains of a sudden headache as she explains that Monica's father wants a divorce.

Several months later she must go down to Berkeley for a few days to appear in court.

"Mother, let me go with you. Please. I promise I'll do whatever you say. Please," Monica begs.

"I wanna go too, then," Gabrielle whines.

"It's not possible," Irina says regretfully. "It's nothing for you to see."

So Irina leaves and the girls stay with Aunt Kathryn. "Shall we go clamming today?" she asks. She takes the girls for a hike and picnic on top of Genessee Island's mountain so they can see how lovely their new home is. She encourages them to try her potter's wheel, which takes concentration, and so their anxieties about their parents are laid aside. At the end of the week they meet Irina at the dock and bring her home to celebrate her return. She is pale and subdued but manages to smile.

"It's nice to be back home again."

The next morning Monica asks the questions she did not dare bring up the night before, when Irina appeared so exhausted. "Mother, what are we going to do now?"

"We'll live here. The Canfields will be in France for two years and so we can stay here in the cottage. The rent isn't too high, so that's good luck."

"I see. But Mother, what will you do? Stay home all day?"

"I wouldn't mind, but I suppose that would never do. Your father will pay child support, although not an awful lot, and I have a little money of my own. Actually, I sold some jewelry that I had put away. I've been thinking I could open a shop. Knitting, crocheting, wools. And I'd call it 'Irina's.' I could teach ballet too. And folksongs. Anything to take in a little cash and while away the time."

That's an odd thing to say; Monica suspects there is something Irina has not yet told her.

"Mother, what's behind this? What do you mean, 'while away the time'?"

Irina takes Monica's hands in her own long, competent ones and looks into Monica's blue eyes. "Have you never heard of divorced people remarrying? It happens all the time. Believe me, one day Josef will come up here and walk in that door and confess that he cannot live without us. And then we will go back."

Can her mother really believe this? Is it an illusion, or is it just possible that Irina has foresight, which she has often claimed, and that Josef will return? Monica doesn't know what to think, but then her mother hasn't asked her opinion either, so she remembers conveniently that she forgot her toothbrush at Kathryn's and breaks away.

4

An Island Child

Monica soon becomes an Island child. At first glance a stranger might think she had always lived there. She and Irina have acquired an ancient bicycle, but it is Monica who uses it most often, exploring the whole Island. She has become one of the most popular baby-sitters and houseworkers for the people who own the expensive houses on the exclusive West Shore.

School is laughably easy and she becomes lazy. It is unlike Monica not to study, but she suspects that being smart in this school would hardly make her popular. For the same reason she never admits that she actually misses the library, concerts, her piano and ballet lessons, foreign movies, and all the bristling discussions she used to have with her Berkeley friends.

Sometimes when she is home alone she goes to the piano, lifts the lid, and begins to play. The piano is more out of tune than ever and Irina keeps saying she will have it tuned, but never does. That shocks Monica less than her fingers, which are losing their flexibility and refuse to perform even those pieces of music she loves very much. A wall seems to arise between her and the piano, and invariably, after a few phrases, she closes the lid over the keyboard and leaves it.

She has made friends, in particular pale blonde Bonnie Robertson, with whom she whispers and exchanges the most personal of confidences. They practice cheerleading together, play flute in the Genessee Marching Band even while they giggle about it, and both resolve to become Festival Queen at the May Festival, which is Genessee Island's big party each year. "It is the greatest honor an Island girl can have," Bonnie says solemnly, and Monica believes this.

One day in early April, a year after Monica has come to the Island, the girls are making fudge in Irina's kitchen, though Irina does not approve of this. Monica's face is losing its smooth fresh quality, and can it be that she is becoming pudgy? Nevertheless, she makes fudge too often. As this particular batch cools, Bonnie says, "Let's go to the drugstore for a Coke. I'll bet Billy and Gene could be down there just about now. Maybe Hal too."

She giggles as she mentions the boys' names.

"Okay," Monica agrees.

As they leave the house, Irina, who has been sitting on the porch rail reading the mail, stops them.

"Monica, I don't want you to go. I have to see you. Alone."

"But I'm going with Bonnie. It can wait till later," Monica replies in an insolent tone that resembles Bonnie's. Irina's green eyes snap; Monica may have been difficult before, but she has never been rude.

"Monica, I want to see you now, and I mean *now*," she says in a steely voice.

Monica sighs audibly and rolls her eyes as if to ask what she can do with this impossible person, her mother. Bonnie goes off by herself, mumbling that she'll see Monica later *if* she can get away.

"Look at you," Irina scolds. "Must you chew gum so loudly—or at all? That's vulgar. And you're slouching."

Irina does not like to scold, but she has been a ballet dancer and can accept nothing but a proud and perfect posture; she is considerably pained by the careless droop that Monica has developed lately and has no patience with it, but controls herself, forcing her tone to be more cordial.

"Monica, a catalogue from a girls' school came today, and I'd like you to look at it."

"Now? Do I have to?"

"Yes, you do. Now."

Resentfully, Monica snatches the catalogue from her

mother's hand and sits on the front steps, strokes her half-grown cat, Louka, and, after an obvious yawn, opens the catalogue.

"The Elizabeth Chatham School for Girls. Well, well, well!" she says with a sarcastic prissiness. The glossy catalogue is sprinkled with photographs showing a procession of girls in cap and gown at graduation, girls riding horses in the morning mist, girl athletes practicing for a swim meet, girls seriously involved in a chemistry experiment in the splendidly furnished lab, and, in order to show that there are lighter moments as well, a scene of girls gathered around a roaring fire in a massive stone fireplace for a midnight snack of hot chocolate and biscuits. Monica gazes for a long time at a simple shot of a girl standing on a stone staircase looking through a leaded glass window; a trick of lighting has the odd effect of making this unknown girl resemble Monica herself. The Main Hall, a rambling half-timber house in Elizabethan style; the library with its leaded glass windows; and the dorms surrounded by rolling lawns and groves of tall firs and cedars might easily be the setting for a novel about a girls' school in England. Dream-book stuff.

"So what's this got to do with me?" Monica asks.

"That's where you're going."

"Where *I'm* going! Mother, are you feeling all right?" Monica has not meant to be rude this time, but a tumult of contradictions is stirring up within her. Once she dreamed of going to such a school, of becoming poised, serene, and even beautiful, like the heroines in the novels she used to read—stories about girls' schools that might have looked very much like this one. Yes, yes, yes, she wants to go there, more than anything else!

But she is afraid, so afraid. Suddenly she sees herself as she thinks her mother sees her, and she hates what she has become—a slob. Her stomach protrudes and she doesn't brush her hair. She would never fit, could never belong to that school with its slender refined girls and its rolling green lawns. She would not dare to go even if she could. No need to worry, she realizes, for there is no way she could get there. No way at all.

"Look, Mother, you're *dreaming*! Look at this page of fees. Good Lord, *look* at it! A thousand for tuition, another thousand for room and board—and that's by the month, is it, or the quarter?—and look at all these other fees. Daddy doesn't even send the child-support checks half the time and you're behind in rent to the Canfields. Please, Mom, be sensible."

Irina takes out her long bone cigarette holder and lights a cigarette—she now allows herself but one a day—and breathes deeply. "I *am* sensible, more sensible than I've ever been, so listen to me, Monica."

"Mother, this is painful for me. I hope you realize this."

Irina pays no attention to her but keeps right on. "You doubtless have not read the fine print about scholarships. They are available to qualified students and everything is paid for—uniform, gym fees, riding lessons, books, the whole thing. And that wonderful uniform, Monica, with the English wool skirts and the blazer with the emblem on the pocket and the darling beret! You'll love it."

Monica's face softens.

"You don't look particularly qualified in those patchy jeans and that skimpy jersey, but you happen to be blessed with a brain. Where it comes from, I'll never know. But every teacher you have ever had has impressed on me the fact that you are one bright girl—very bright, in fact. We can't have you wasting away here. Even your teacher here tells me that."

"You want to get rid of me, is that it?" Monica asks sullenly, suspecting it might be true.

"Of course not, my darling. You don't really believe *that*, do you? It's just that this school is better for you than the school here on the Island. Besides, I'm afraid you're beginning to act just like Bonnie."

"And what's wrong with Bonnie?" She is insolent again.

"Nothing where she's concerned. But I don't like to see you imitating her. You're too fine, Monica, too bright. If only you knew how lucky you are!"

"Ha ha!" Monica says unpleasantly. Why is she so rude? Irina is trying so hard to help her, and yet she blocks her at every step. Monica leaves the porch and sits on the swing under an enormous tree in the yard, sits there twisting the rope and wishing she were someone else, an entirely different person with a different name and different parents and, above all, a better personality.

How she wants to go away to this school! There she can at least pretend she is someone else. Yet the others will know, those rich girls who don't have to depend on scholarships and whose parents are possibly comforting "Mumsy and Papa" instead of a stubborn violinist and an eccentric Hungarian, both of them gypsies in their way. No, she will never be accepted. Surprisingly, Monica finds something else, too, blocking her way—a reluctance at the thought of leaving her mother and Gabrielle and Bittersweet Place, which has become home.

Irina pays no attention to her objections and fears

but fills out application blanks, sees that Monica takes the necessary tests, and makes appointments for her to appear for personal interviews in Vancouver, where the school is located.

It is while she is riding on the bus to one of these required interviews that Monica remembers her father's having told her about several favorite concerts he has given in Vancouver, which is a musical city, "One of my favorite places," he once remarked. Possibly he might give another concert there, and it's possible that he might visit her then. Monica cannot quite believe, as Irina still does, that Josef will come to the Island, but if he should come to Vancouver, surely he would want to see her. This new hope leaps up within her like a fish jumping into the sunlight. She does brilliantly at the interviews and becomes a minor sensation on the Island when she is awarded a full scholarship.

One crisp morning in September Monica waits on the dock for *The Genessee Queen* to take her to the mainland. At a central place in Vancouver, the school limousine will meet her and take her to the Chatham School, which is located a few miles north of the center of the city.

A small crowd gathers for the send-off. Gabrielle jumps up and down with excitement; Aunt Kathryn glows; Jim Weed, who has become one of Irina's admirers, has a gift for Monica; and some of Monica's school friends make feeble jokes and wisecracks. As Monica stands self-conscious and proud in the handsome new uniform, she wishes that Irina made a better appearance; a toothache has swollen her cheek and the wool scarf she has tied around her head is meant to be fashionable, but instead gives her a dismal ghetto air. Yet her eyes shine as she flicks an imaginary hair from the navy blazer of her daughter's uniform.

Even to the very end, Monica refuses to let her mother know how happy she is about going to this unbelievable school. This reluctance is mysterious and may have something to do with that last tiny knot of resentment she feels toward Irina for having left Josef. Yet she is touched when Irina wreathes her long slender arms around her daughter.

"Let me kiss you good-bye, Monica. I'm so proud of you, so awfully proud. Work hard now, but have some fun too. And write to me when you arrive, so I'll know that you got there. A card will be enough. We'll miss you so much, but Christmas isn't so far away, and you'll come home then . . ."

Monica kisses her mother and thanks everyone for their kind words and good-luck wishes. Soon she is waving from the deck of the ferry as it moves away from the Island, but she refuses to let the tears come until *The Genessee Queen* turns the bend and there is no fear of being seen. Again she is in a tumult of conflict; if only she had been kinder to Irina, who is so good; she does not really want to leave the Island, for it will never be the same again for her; and oh she is frightened about school—will she be smart enough, and will the other girls like her, and can she somehow transform herself into a new Monica Kroll? She is full of fears; yet before the ferry even reaches the mainland, she begins to smile and cannot stop, for she is on her own now and it is very exciting indeed.

PART ONE

Going Home to Genessee

1

A Friday in May
Two Years Later

The holiday weekend has begun.

At the moment it is a blue day, everything blue, so blue that Monica feels herself drenched in blueness. She leans on the rail of *The Genessee Queen* as it leaves the mainland and wonders that she has never tired of the trip, though she has made it many times. She knows exactly how the cool northern light will bathe the islands that rise in the distance, how it will turn the water a gunmetal-blue. A ferry that sails in the distance and the gulls screeching mournfully as they circle above remain insistently white. Yet possibly all the blueness will turn to gray and the color will drain away as if the whole view were an overexposed film negative, for the sun lurks among a furrow of moody clouds.

"Please let it be nice weather!" Monica pleads. The three May Festivals that she has seen have taken place under moody skies, but this Festival weekend will be different. For three weeks now she has known the amazing news. Her father is coming to the Island! Irina was right after all.

The wind is chilling and the salt spray is drenching her uniform, but Monica prefers to stand here on the deck—it's been so long since she's had the chance to be alone. Finally she walks inside to the warm cabin and picks her way between the sprawling legs of holiday-bound students sitting in the aisles and their backpacks, lumps of green and orange canvas strewn over the floor. On other trips home, when she changed to jeans before leaving school, she often wormed her way into these chattering groups, and even today, filled as she is with the excitement of her father's coming, she could do with a good laugh or some flirting. Yet she also needs to be alone, so she makes her way to the front of the cabin and watches the flat silhouettes of the islands in the distance become green with firs and cedars as the *Queen* passes them and then retreat into gray stillness again.

"Home for the holidays, dear?"

She might have known someone would want to talk with her, for the school uniform never fails to attract at least one genteel soul like this Kindly Passenger, who smiles with that easy Canadian friendliness that Monica often admires but also despairs of at times—such as now—when she would prefer to be alone. Still, this is a pleasant old dear, and it would be unkind to move away.

"Yes," Monica answers simply and politely, without inviting conversation.

"You must be so happy! There's nothing like going home on holiday, is there, after months of school?"

Monica agrees. It would be too difficult to explain that anyone who has many homes has no home, and she has many homes. The school is home, the Island is home, and now that her father is coming, visions of La Californie, the Berkeley house, renew themselves, and she wonders if that is her real home. For three weeks now she has dreamed of going back again to that house that was always full of people and the sound of music. Will the lemon tree in the patio have grown? Will the deer still come down from the Berkeley hills? Will she dare to sit at the grand piano once more and learn to play again?

The friendly lady, snug in her knit scarf and hat, warm and toasty as a cup of hot tea and a bun at four o'clock on a damp afternoon, doesn't notice Monica's hesitation and continues with her chat.

"And you'll be so glad to see Mother and Dad again!" she assumes.

Dear lady, that's a touchy question! Monica smiles, says nothing.

"Of course, I can tell you're from the Chatham School. Lucky girl! My grandniece went there, had the time of her life—sailing, swimming, dramatics, hockey . . . and she *studied* too. Worked hard. She says her years there were the happiest of her life!"

Hooray for her, Monica thinks with some irony while she smiles and gives a nod that means yes. She might even have agreed with the Kindly Passenger were this her first year. But the pleasant lady sees it from a distance, through the pages of the catalogue, as it were, and Monica has had a closer experience, has witnessed scenes that will never be photographed for publicity. Chatham is a good school, no doubt about that, yet she has been longing to go back to Berkeley; there is a quickness there that Chatham lacks. Still, the Kindly Passenger is not really speaking to Monica; she is addressing the school uniform—the plaid skirt, the navy blazer with its ornate gilt emblem on the pocket, the white tailored shirt and striped school tie. If she were to wear her jeans, chances are this woman and others like her would look past her as though she didn't really exist.

"There's nothing like a good English school for girls, and this one has transplanted well to the Canadian West, hasn't it? Enjoy it, my dear. These are your best years." The dear soul smiles.

Shall I tell her, Monica wonders, about one student who only yesterday attempted suicide, or of the many girls who are sent to Chatham because they are clearly not wanted at home or because it's awkward to have a young girl around when her parents are going through a divorce? Can anyone count the tears that are shed silently at night on dormitory pillows? Yet there *are* moments that quiver with poignancy, brief intensities that Monica treasures.

At this point a tall white-haired man with pale blue eyes and a cap of Scottish tweed steps up to tell his wife that within five minutes—he takes a watch from his pocket and shows her to prove it—the ferry will be stopping at Galiano Island.

"Oh my, I'd better hurry, then," the Kindly Passenger says. "I've been having such a nice chat with this lovely young lady. Tell me, Harry, have you ever seen such deep blue eyes? And that wonderful thick dark hair! She's a Chatham girl, isn't that nice? Have a nice holiday, dear!" she finishes, patting Monica's hand before she turns to leave with Harry.

"It's been nice talking with you too," Monica answers, and she finds that she really means it, for somehow she senses that it must be remarkable to reach the age of seventy or eighty and retain a sweetness of spirit.

How tender this old couple is, she thinks, as they

move together toward the lower deck, how considerate of each other! Have they been married for years and years and years? She thinks so. It is a miracle.

2

What Monica Did Not Tell the Kindly Passenger

What Monica has been unable to tell the Kindly Passenger or anyone is that for the past three weeks she has been trembling in a confusion of ecstasy, fear, and hope because she will soon be seeing her father. Irina wrote her this amazing news, and Monica had to shake her head and smile, because only Irina would mention it casually in a P.S. following a long chatty letter in her big impulsive handwriting in which she discussed Louka's new kittens, a new recipe for carrot cake, a possible increase in taxes, and rumors about the Tilson girl running off with a man from Richmond. Then, after all this, a postscript. "Guess who will be giving a concert here during the Festival weekend? A trio. Yes, the Josef Kroll Trio with the Great Josef himself! And why not, eh?"

In all this time Monica has heard from her father only once, in a letter one of the University secretaries typed in answer to the note she sent him when she received her scholarship at Chatham.

Dearest Monica,

Great news! Congratulations on your scholarship! It will be hard not to boast of my fine bright girl. I can hardly believe you have become so grown-up that you are actually going away to school!

Please forgive me for not having written to you very much. I love you now as I always have loved you, but letter-writing is not one of my virtues.

My best wishes to you in your new venture,

With all my love,

Your father, Josef

Monica read the letter over and over and kissed it and held it close to her bosom like a silly actress in an early sentimental movie. Immediately she forgave him for the telephone calls he hadn't answered, the letters he hadn't written, and even the child-support checks he'd often forgotten, although this particular neglect filled Irina with despair as she wondered how they would get through the month. Yet they made excuses for Josef: he is an artist, inclined to be forgetful; he is heedless as a child. But he loves them, and someday he will come to take them back. Monica *believes* he will come to take her back.

Is that really why he is coming to the Island? Is the concert only an excuse?

It is clear to Monica that most likely her mother is behind this idea. She has managed to be elected to the Festival Committee, some of the members of which want to see Culture on the Island, and surely she has planted the idea of an impressive concert in their heads.

Yet certain questions cannot be put aside. Why should Irina care about Josef's coming now that the divorce is nearly three years old? Why should Josef take the trouble to make this long trip when the Kroll Trio is already well known and most likely does not need this concert? The thought keeps leaping up in her mind that he wants to take her home . . . but possibly he is only curious about Irina and his daughters. And she is curious too. What will he be like after all this time?

"Is that really your father? Wow, he's gorgeous!"

"Is he a movie star? An old one, I mean? One of the great lovers. Ha ha!"

"He doesn't have to be in the movies. He's famous already, one of the best violinists in the world!" Sheila, Monica's roommate, boasts, almost as if Josef were *her* father.

The girls in Monica's room at the dorm are commenting on this dated, professionally touched-up photograph of Josef.

"Monica, you are the only person I know who has a picture of her father on the wall of her room. The only one I can think of. Everyone else has pictures of a mother, boyfriends, horses, dogs, but never a father."

"Yeah, I keep mine tucked away at the bottom of my sweater drawer."

"I have a snapshot of my father, but I don't even know where it is."

"You can't trust parents. Only horses are safe. Give me horses any time."

"Keep your horse. I'll keep my boyfriends on my wall."

"Can't trust boyfriends either. They become husbands and fathers."

Monica is not rare in being a child of divorce, for more than half the girls have parents long since separated. Fathers tend to be forgotten, and here Monica stands alone, for she has given her father's photograph, no matter how false it may be, a place of honor on her wall. She has inherited his deep blue eyes, whereas Gabrielle's are sparkling green like her mother's. "A deep and sometimes melancholy blue" is how she thinks of Josef's eyes, and the photographer has not been able to alter this.

"Don't you have a picture of your mother?" somebody asks.

"She wouldn't have room for it, this photograph is so big."

Monica does not say anything. For the first time it occurs to her that she has no formal portrait of her mother, only a snapshot in which Irina holds a cherubic Monica on a beach in France, or is it Greece? . . . somewhere where the sun is so bright that the lights in the snapshot are too light and the shadows are far too dark. The Irina who smiles into the camera is very young, and she sparkles. Monica keeps this picture casually in the back of a French-English dictionary, as if it were not important at all.

Sheila prattles on about Josef's career and insists once more that "everyone knows about Josef Kroll, one of the most famous violinists in the world." Monica smiles secretly at this extravagance, as if Sheila knew anything about it. Monica knows this is not even remotely true, yet she grew up believing that her father was *the* great violinist of the century.

> *"Why, both David Oistrakh and Yehudi Menu-hin begged your father to give them lessons," Irina told her when she was a very little girl, wide-eyed and impressionable. Her father's blue eyes twin-kled as he agreed with Irina's story. It wasn't until she was twelve that she realized she had been the butt of a joke and that her father was considered in musical circles as good enough but hardly ex-traordinary.*

"Why had her parents told her so many stories, so many little lies?" she wonders. Perhaps because she be-lieved them so readily.

> *"Tell me about the gypsies who stole you when you were a little boy in Hungary," she used to beg, and her father would embroider one tale after an-other about growing up in a gypsy world after an ancient gypsy queen recognized the mark of the violinist on him and stole him from his home.*

Of course those stories came to an end when she found out on a visit to her grandmother in the Bronx that her father had been only one of hundreds of precocious young violinists in New York and that for a long time he had earned his living dressed as a gypsy violinist, performing in the better Rumanian and Hungarian restaurants in New York.

Yet in a sense he really was a gypsy. For until the house in Berkeley, Monica's entire life had been spent moving from one place to another—Amsterdam, Paris, Nice, Rochester, New York, Montreal, Iowa, Avignon . . . back and forth and never resting as he made a concert tour here or got a teaching fellowship there.

> *One hot August day that summer they spent in the south of France she was driving with her father through country roads when they came upon a mansion that she loved immediately.*
>
> *"Look at that house there!" she cried.*
>
> *"No wonder you like it," Josef answered. "It's La Californie. Picasso used to live there."*
>
> *"I wish I could."*
>
> *"We can do better than that. How about going to California?"*
>
> *He could offer this extravagant promise because he had just signed a contract for a position at the University. The very next month they were living in a house hardly comparable to the French estate yet superb, for it was theirs. A white house, vaguely Spanish, with arched windows, a red tiled roof, and a patio where lemon trees grew. It was her mother who painted the sign that announced it as* La Californie.

After her mother's letter came, she dreamed that Josef came to the Island to tell her that his real reason for coming was to take her back to La Californie. She is quite sure that he did not mention Irina or Gabrielle in the dream, so perhaps he is undecided about them. The dream shows vividly that Josef wants her, entirely and without question. Yet in her waking moments she sometimes wonders if she can trust a dream. It is a wish, not a promise. And yet she wants so much to go back to California with her father that every time she thinks of it she is aware of a fluttering deep down inside herself, as though she were ready to fly.

——3
Sheila

It is so unbelievable that the very next day, in less than twenty-four hours, she will be seeing her father, that Monica wants nothing to interrupt her joy. And yet the image of Sheila haunts her, Sheila weeping until her eyes are red and her nose is moist and dripping . . .

Monica is packed and ready to leave, afraid she will miss the ferry if she doesn't hurry. Yet she cannot simply walk out on her roommate.

"But Monica, you promised I could come to visit you during the May Festival. Don't you remember? You promised! You gave me your word. And now you're breaking your promise."

"Sheila, dear Sheila, listen to me. Try to understand. I invited you to Genessee before I knew that my father was coming home. I only found out three weeks ago. For one thing, our cottage is small, there won't be any room, and besides, it will be kind of a private family gathering. You wouldn't want to butt in on that."

"Yes, I would!"

She is practically sticking out her tongue and stamping her foot like a six-year-old having a temper tantrum. What is Monica to do with her?

She looks out the window as she waits for Sheila to end her latest sobs. Below, three girls are walking across the lawn, which the afternoon sun has lit with an emerald edge. How lighthearted they are, laughing over some quip one of them has made! A picture from the Chatham School catalogue. Yet here is Sheila, still angry.

"You don't want me and my own parents don't want me and nobody at school wants me," she cries, and unfortunately it is so true that Monica hardly knows what to answer. Still, Sheila is her responsibility; she would help her if she knew how.

"Sheila, there are millions of things you can do this vacation. Maybe you can get your folks to take you on a trip somewhere. What about Hawaii? If not, there are lots of things going on right here in Vancouver. And I do promise you can come and stay with me a whole week, later on, if you like. And I won't have to break that promise."

Sheila sits on her bed, no longer crying, but a strand of hair hangs over her face and she does not say anything. The chimes ring out and Monica says, "I have to go now; I can't wait any longer. Please try to understand," she begs.

But Sheila only looks up at her as her eyes fill with accusing tears and she does not say yes or no.

"I do care about you, Sheila," Monica assures her, and as she says it, realizes that this is true. But something must be done about her, and it grieves her that she hasn't the slightest idea what that might be.

"I'll try to call you over the weekend," she says in desperation as she hurries out of the room.

Last September when Monica returned to school, expecting to room with the bright, dark-eyed Laura Hyatt, another scholarship student (with whom she had founded the famous and infamous—and thoroughly illegal—Midnight Club, which met for discussions in the dorm), she found a note asking her to see the headmistress at once.

"But what have I done?" Monica worried. Had the school decided not to renew her scholarship—a constant fear—or was something wrong at home? Had they found out about the Midnight Club? Nervously she brushed her long dark hair, straightened her uniform, and asked Laura if she could borrow her school tie, as hers was packed away somewhere in her luggage.

For ten minutes of increasing anguish Monica waited outside Miss Dryden's office. Finally the headmistress, cool and poised, greeted her with a gracious smile and offered her a chair inside the office. "She is making it easy for me," Monica thought, "because something terrible is bound to come." After a proper amount of routine chitchat, Miss Dryden came to the point . . .

She leans forward and her voice drops so that it cannot possibly be overheard. "This could be a spy movie," Monica thinks.

"I know that you and Laura planned to room together, but I'm afraid we'll have to change that. You see, both of you are here not only for your fine grades, but also for the good influence you will have on our regular students."

She punctuates this with a small dry smile and a nod

of the head. Monica waits, expecting the worst, and the worst is what she gets.

"Monica, we would like you to room with Sheila Dawes. You know her, don't you?"

"The girl who has no friends" is how Monica thinks of her, but she clears her throat and mumbles a yes, Miss Dryden.

"You understand that our little talk here is confidential. Sheila is not very happy, although nobody knows why, but it was thought that if she could be in the company of someone who is as vital and stable as you that she might grow into the kind of young woman we like to see at Elizabeth Chatham."

Monica cannot very well object to being considered "vital and stable," but she thinks that the truth is that she has a quixotic personality. She often bursts into tears without knowing why and she can laugh herself into a fit over nothing at all. She is anything but affirmative. And to think of giving up wonderful Laura for this pale and watery drip of a girl!

"Sheila's parents are very eager to see Sheila become happier, or at least more like the other girls. If you do room with her, you may be given special privileges on occasion; that is, if you would like to go to a play or concert with Sheila, or if she should invite you home for a weekend, it can be arranged. And of course it doesn't mean that if you room with Sheila you won't see Laura. She'll be there in the dorm."

Monica begins to realize she won't be able to get out of this.

"You may or may not be aware, Monica, that Sheila's parents have contributed handsomely to the school fund and have mentioned something about helping us out with the new gym, so of course we should like to see Sheila succeed here."

Not being the least bit stupid, Monica translates this bit of newsy chatter as Miss Dryden has intended she should. Scholarships such as Monica's depend on the kind of contributions grateful parents, like the Daweses, are apt to make. Monica could insist on rooming with Laura, for it has already been arranged, but she may pay heavily for it.

"In the long run, you may find that rooming with Sheila may be of real value to you—in more ways than one," Miss Dryden remarks. "And so, you are willing to try this new arrangement?"

"Yes," Monica says meekly.

"I'm so glad. It's a task you are taking on, I don't deny that, but I think you may succeed. And if you wish to come and talk with me at any time, please do so. All our girls are important."

She coughs delicately and nods to show that the interview has come to an end. Monica shakes the hand that is offered to her.

"Thank you, Miss Dryden. I'll do what I can."

Sheila adores Monica immediately and begs her to spend a weekend at her home, located in one of the wealthy old-fashioned sections of Vancouver. Unable to refuse her without hurting her feelings, Monica goes home with her one Friday afternoon.

"What a great setting for a movie!" Monica remarks as she first views the extensive brown-shingled Victorian house surrounded by gloomy cedars and deodars. The setting for an old-fashioned murder mystery or a Charles Addams cartoon, she thinks, but there's no point in mentioning this, for it would be lost on Sheila. Besides, as Mr. Dawes' long black car approaches the house, Sheila seems to shrink back into the leather seat.

The interior of the house is hardly a surprise, being proper, dark, and uninspired except for a portrait of a handsome young man over the fireplace; proper spotlights are focused on it. Photographs of the same young man can be seen on the other walls and in expensive leather frames on tables and in the front hall and over the sideboard . . . everywhere. Mrs. Dawes, a small, nasal-voiced woman, is pleased that Monica notices the portrait, and is only too happy to rush with explanations.

"That is George Phillip, our son. Sheila's big brother." She sighs.

"He's very handsome," Monica remarks.

"Handsome, brilliant, charming, promising . . . there wasn't a good quality he didn't have," Mrs. Dawes says, her eyes focused on the portrait. "He was going to Cambridge, you know; friends invited him on a mountain-climbing trip and he went, willy-nilly, as young men will do. There was a storm; he fell and later passed away."

"I'm sorry," Monica says.

She does not add that Sheila has never once mentioned a brother and that even now, as her mother praises George Phillip, she sits miserably on the edge of her chair and looks down at her stubby school shoes.

The weekend lasts forever. The sparse conversation is directed at Monica for the most part. Mr. Dawes, retired, shows Monica his gem collection and pebble-polishing machine. Mrs. Dawes complains of her responsibilities as president of the Ladies' Guild at church. Nobody kisses, hugs, or even touches anyone else. At last Mr. Dawes backs the long black car out of his driveway and takes the girls back to school.

"I'm sorry it was so deadly, so dull, so *goddamn* boring," Sheila says.

It is unlike Sheila to use such strong language, but Monica understands why she must do so. She also understands why Sheila insisted on her going home for a weekend though she knew it could only be boring. It was her way of providing Monica with the clues to the mystery of why such obviously rich people should live such bleak lives and have produced such a lost and desolate Sheila.

"I get it, but what am *I* supposed to do about it at this point?" Monica wonders.

The next week she decides that she can trust Sheila to go with her to the Midnight Club and makes her promise she will not breathe a word of it to anyone. Sheila is exuberantly happy with the invitation and promises, "You can cut out my tongue if I so much as mention it."

"I will," Monica threatens, but she is smiling because Sheila is so pleased.

On that particular night as they sit in Laura's room and sip beer that someone has mysteriously "found," the eight girls who are present drift into a discussion of what they will do when they are finished with school. Doctor, lawyer, secretary, teacher, air hostess . . . everyone but Sheila has an answer, but it is Monica's decision that jars everyone.

"I shall marry a rich man and let him take care of

me the rest of my life. Live a life of ease! Strawberries
and cream! A Rolls-Royce! Whatever!"

"How cynical!"

"Not cynical. She's just been believing all those old
movies from the Thirties."

"I just can't believe you really mean it, Monica.
You're not that naïve."

"But I do mean it," Monica insists. "It's not all that
farfetched."

"Do you have someone in mind? I'll bet you do.
Come on, Monica, who is it? You can tell us."

"No comment!" Monica laughs. "Actually there is
someone, but my lips are sealed."

The discussion expands, becomes more philosophic,
and Sheila grins with enjoyment although she is too shy
to say a word. Yet later that night, as she and Monica
lie in their narrow beds, she confesses that she is puzzled.

"Monica, I think the girls could be right. It's ridiculous to think about marrying a man just because he's
rich. Rich people can be awful—not all of them, of
course, but some. Like my father. He's not super-rich
but he's rich enough, and you know what a bore our life
is."

"He pays the bills, doesn't he? You never have to
worry about paying rent, or getting a new pair of shoes
if you want them, or going to a concert or the theater if
you should happen to think you'd like to. Money, dear
Sheila, is not necessarily such bad stuff."

"But you could make a mistake, Monica," she says
softly. This is the first time that Sheila does not entirely
agree with Monica, and Monica is gratified. This is an
improvement. Besides, what would Sheila know about

money troubles? She could not possibly understand what they are.

"Do you really have someone in mind, Monica?" Sheila asks.

"Yes." Monica laughs and hopes she sounds mysterious. "Good night now; let's get some sleep before six o'clock comes around."

The months have flown by since that particular conversation and Monica has witnessed an awareness in Sheila, and a growing confidence, that wasn't there before. A slight improvement at most. But now, as she sits in the cabin of the ferry as it churns across the water, Sheila seems to her only a spoiled child, a problem to be dealt with. And she couldn't possibly have taken her home, not this weekend. "I'll make it up to her somehow," she promises herself.

4

The Story of My Life, Miss Cornwall

Monica moves to one of the back seats of the cabin of the ferry and, crowded though it is, she feels a quiet space around her. Two little girls, blonde and pudding-faced, stare up at her and then disappear to run wildly around the cabin, shouting and carefree. For a moment she wishes she were one of them, would gladly change places. She is ecstatic about seeing her father; yet the foghorn from a passing ship seems to warn, "Beware, beware!"

As if being haunted with guilt about Sheila were not enough, she is plagued intermittently with the memory that the autobiography required for Miss Cornwall's English course is due at the end of the holiday, next Wednesday.

"Stupid thing!" she says as she opens her notebook to the page where the assignment is clearly outlined. This is the first paper that has ever baffled her, yet it should be the easiest of requirements to finish. Nor can it be disregarded, for she will not go on to her senior year unless this is completed. It is her habit to work with fastidious energy; she has often finished papers before they are due and more than once she has been praised for her work, which is orderly, logical, and sometimes brilliant.

"But this is too much!" she cries silently, unable to understand what's wrong.

Once more she sees Miss Cornwall giving out the assignment, and that was last September, eight months ago! Mild Miss Cornwall with the gray eyes flashing behind her bifocals explains in modulated tones, in perfect and impersonal English, exactly what is to be done:

"The subject of this very important paper is yourself. It will be the story of your life up to the present, generally speaking, but you will be allowed a certain latitude in the way you treat it. I expect more than a chronological listing of events. You may want to find a theme or motif that seems characteristic of your life and build your autobiography around that. The title that you choose may give you a clue. It will take time and thought, but of course it is not due until after the Victoria Day vacation."

Good, Monica thinks as she writes down the requirements. She expects to draft her paper one week and
type it the next and so be done with it.

"Now, then," Miss Cornwall continues, "certain matters should be treated—in your own style, of course.
Your place of birth, your background, your parents and
their influence as you see it, the history of your education, influences in your life, the subjects that you enjoy
the most, and, finally, what you plan to do with your
life. I expect that you will include anything else that
appeals to you as being important. Are there any questions?" she ends cheerfully.

"Oh, Miss Cornwall, do I have a question!" Monica
thinks. "But there's no point in asking if you'd really
like to know why my life is such a mess."

Before the class is over, three disparate images, or
memories, or glimpses of the past, as sharply defined as
though they were on a film in front of her, dart in and
out of her mind—things she has forgotten long ago.

>   *She is in Nice with her father and he is selecting
>   fruit at the open market, carefully comparing one
>   deep purple bunch of grapes with another, his
>   hands full of the perfect fruit and his eyes filled
>   with admiration for them.*
>
>   *She sees an apartment in Rome that was once a
>   palace and she sees herself in the morning as she
>   wears a white nightgown; her mother braids her
>   hair and the sound of her father practicing his vio-
>   lin sings through the lavish rooms. But another
>   image follows immediately:*
>
>   *A nightmare recollection of the street in Brook-
>   lyn where her mother grew up, the marked walls*

and filthy stairs that lead to her grandmother's apartment. The smell of poverty.

Sitting there in the class she shudders to think of this last image.

"Enough of that," she tells herself sternly as she goes to the next class. "That sort of thing won't get me anywhere."

And yet when she least expects it—in the locker room at gym, or in the middle of dessert in the dining hall, or on her way back from the tennis courts after a game—fragments of the past blink across her vision. But surely this is not what Miss Cornwall has in mind.

That weekend she determines to work directly and purposefully. And her notebook now contains notes she may possibly use.

BEGINNINGS: Ordinary and miraculous, as a sperm unites with an egg.

Still, it was highly unexpected—though knowing Irina's ways, probably inevitable. My father used to "court" my mother (that old-fashioned phrase is decidedly his, not mine) after performances of an opera company (possibly third-rate, certainly not the Met); he was concertmaster and she was a member of the corps de ballet. Much dancing and revelry for both of them, romantic walks through the park, so they tell me, a fiery romance. When poor Irina learned I was materializing in a way that could no longer be ignored, my father gallantly or willingly or helplessly married her, so that my entrance into the world was legitimate.

It was a quaint and thoughtful gesture. It's how they took care of those things at that time.

Immediately she crosses this out. It will never do.

Monica thinks again, now, that Miss Cornwall would relish this information. But she is certain that she would show it to Miss Dryden "as her duty compels." She, Monica, may have to fudge a bit, perhaps describe a stage wedding? Yet if she begins that she will have to make up a complete fiction about some mythical Monica Kroll. She lets that go for now and reads what else she has written.

BACKGROUND.

The word stands alone but she has thought of what she might have written.

Why must everybody know? She has to fill out many applications and inevitably her father has been angry.

"What does it mean, this religion, this nationality? Pieces of paper, that's all. Ask my religion and I will tell you; music is my religion, all the religion I need. I pray through music. What else does anyone need? If music were religion, we might have arguments about tonalities or modes, whatever you like, but not wars with guns and bombs and killing.

"Nationality. That's even more stupid. Monica, put down that you are Hungarian on both sides with a touch of Russian, a Greek grandmother, a Jewish great-grandfather, a pinch of French, an

Armenian cousin, certainly a touch of Italian. This is all true, and what does it mean? Can you tell which part of you is which?"

Irina steps in. "All right, Josef, for heaven's sake. You are giving lectures to the poor child. Look, Monica, you are American, born in Manhattan. Your father comes from the Bronx and I come from Brooklyn. That's all you have to say. It's enough. Anything more is nobody's business."

"I suppose I'll have to write that I'm American, plain American, but Miss Cornwall would prefer me to be English," she muses as the ferry lurches, letting off passengers at another small island. "Perhaps I should invent a proper Canadian Monica, of British background of course, something that can be traced back to 1066; Sundays at the Anglican Church and summers on the West Shore of Genessee." She is afraid that's what they want.

The next page is blank except for the one-word heading EDUCATION. Once more she thinks of what she might write, were she to tell the truth.

There's a tangle if there ever was one.

Experimental preschool in Massachusetts where she learned numbers and colors so that even now when she sees a three she sees it fat and rosy; four is cerulean blue; five is golden, of course; six is a shy violet; and seven is crimson. This experiment was later abandoned, but for Monica numbers still glow and equations resemble abstract paintings.

In Avignon the convent school with the nuns' skirts whipping in the morning breeze and herself in a blue smock as she learns to read and write in French. Sister Dominique is her first love, the only person in all this world who ever taught her a prayer.

It was Irina, of course, who sought out the best schools. In England it was an experimental school where she rode her bicycle to a chilly farmhouse in the country; school was playing the recorder and milking the goats and making watery vegetarian soups. In Dubrovnik a series of private teachers. In Italy an American school where she could hardly understand a word the teacher said, not because of language difficulties but because the teacher talked as if she had a hot potato in her mouth.

At last two blessed years, the last one interrupted, in an ordinary public school—which, of course, was anything but ordinary for her, that school in Berkeley only four blocks away from La Californie.

As for the school in Genessee . . .

She can hardly think of anything kind to say about it, but on the whole this section may develop. Still, how can it be told? To sit under a chestnut tree beside Sister Dominique and embroider while the nun reads stories and the sun makes dappled shadows on the ground! Or the frustration of being accused of copying a story she knows she has written by herself, especially when she could not quite tell what the idiotic teacher in the Italian school was saying! Or the way the wind nipped her nose and froze her knees as she piped her recorder while skipping through a pasture at that unbelievable English school. This is what she remembers.

Anyway, it was music that counted. Her father saw to that. And why does it hurt to write it down when it is so important?

FAVORITE SUBJECTS

A sterile classification. As if music were a subject! "Music is part of life, like air or water, and without it I cannot live," Monica thinks as she gazes through the steamy windows of the ferry and sees nothing. She glances at her notebook once more. "All right, Miss Cornwall."

> MATH. Something I appreciate because two and two are four and it is a consolation to know they will never amount to three or five, or so we believe. One of the few facts in this world one can trust. Math has the same kind of truth that music does, but at some points they follow different directions.

> CHEMISTRY. H_2O is water and I am glad because that much, simple as it is, is fairly stable. Chemistry tries to know what it can test, not what it dreams of . . . or so I think . . . but then I am aghast at the frightful things that chemists have dreamed. Poisons, gases, such murderous things that I cannot love chemistry after all, cannot trust the chemists.

> PSYCHOLOGY. This has not yet been offered, but I am curious about what it will be like. Also doubtful, or if that's too strong a term, then let us say questioning. Can people be captured in a silence?

Or would poetry perhaps tell us more accurately what we need to know?

Monica scratches three crosses through this section. What would Miss Cornwall say, or Miss Dryden, and above all what would the Scholarship Committee think?

WHAT DO YOU WISH TO MAKE OF YOUR LIFE?

Still another blank page. She dreams:

It is early morning and she sits at the piano in her nightgown. Was it Rome, Nice? No, it was Montreal, because outside the snow was coming down in slow wet flakes. Then she hears the sound of a violin accompanying her early Bach gavotte, and she looks up and smiles to see her father nodding at her as he improvises a melody. It is the first time he has done this and it is the most wonderful thing she has ever experienced.

"Ha!" he cries when they have finished. "My new accompanist!"

As she begins another little piece, he bends down and kisses her on "her kissing place," which is the back of her neck. She laughs deliciously and later tells her mother that when she grows up she will play the piano for Daddy "forever and forever and forever."

So much for that! Begin again; what will you do with your life?

One of the things I wish to do in this life, yes, what I wish to make of my life, is to be married to a rich man who adores me.

She slumps in her seat, hands over her eyes. So far she has thought of nothing she can use. Perhaps two autobiographies are in order, one of them an expurgated edition for Miss Cornwall, full of dates and facts. The other will float with images.

It's too bad, but hardly amazing, that Miss Cornwall did not include love affairs among the headings.

> FIRST LOVE. *That dark-haired boy on the beach one day in June. Dubrovnik. He could say, "Hello, Monica," and she could say, "Sdravo, Milo." Monica and Milo. She can still feel the brush of his lips on hers. They ran along the beach, built a castle in the sand, kissed each other again and again, and cried when it was time for Monica to move somewhere else with her father and mother.*

"Miss Cornwall, I don't think you would like that, but then again you might," Monica decides. Why is this such a puzzle? Why can't she get anywhere with it?

She slams the notebook shut and walks to the front of the cabin, where she peers out over the pewter-gray water and sees Genessee Island rising in the distance.

5

Courtney Phillips, or, Someday I Shall Marry a Rich Man

"I won't think about the bio again, not any of it, until the Festival is over," she decides, and wisely too, because otherwise she will show her worries on her face and her father will not like it. He has always preferred pretty women and lighthearted girls.

She orders her thinking mind to rest and becomes a camera moving through blue and green waters. A flock of cormorants flies over the waves—and there, one sweeps down into the water and rises again with a fish in its mouth.

"I love it all," she thinks, "the water, the islands, the skies." They have already passed that tiny island on which someone has built a single dwelling that resembles a small Japanese temple. And off to the right another island appears; if she squints her eye just so, it resembles a girl sleeping, reminds her of Sheila. Something important about Sheila shimmers through the mist, something she might do, but she cannot think it through because a masculine hand rests on her shoulder and the pale image of Sheila vanishes. Monica turns around to see Courtney grinning at her. Immediately she whips off her glasses—how she hates those frames!—and smiles up warmly.

"Now that we're practically there, I find you. Where have you *been* all this time?" he asks.

"Right here. Wondering if you'd show up. How are you, Court?"

He answers by hugging her, a properly affectionate hug since he is intensely aware that they are in full view of everyone in the cabin, but his hand lingers on hers. What a perfect young man he is—so very perfect that she must get used to it every time she sees him! Are you a mirage, Monica once asked him, and so he had to hug her and hold her very close and tight to prove how finite he was. Brown wavy hair, eyes of uncompromising blue, and perfect vision, perfect teeth, not even a pimple anywhere, but a nose that juts out in an aggressive way, which is surprising, for he does not appear to be aggressive in the least. Perhaps he hides it? His clothes, of course—professional tennis sweater over well-cut cords—are impeccable.

"You look superb, Mon. Stretching out or something?"

"A little," she says in pleased embarrassment. She has grown several inches taller this year; her waist has slimmed; Irina claims she is "budding" and should be proud of it. There has never been a flat chest in her family!

"How's college?" Monica asks. "Exams coming up?"

"Now don't spoil the holiday, Monica. Yes, they're lurking in wait," he whispers. "Let's let them lurk!"

"That's exactly what I've decided." She laughs. "Is this your first trip to the Island this year?"

"No, Dad and I came up last month to open the house and work on the boat. Of course, we open it 'officially' this weekend."

"Great!" she says, thinking how pleasant it must be to talk so blithely of opening and closing houses for the season. "And how is the boat?"

He talks in technical terms, filling her in with more details than she can absorb, but she can imagine Court and his father working together in the garage of Skiffington, which is the name of the substantial West Shore house where the Phillipses spend their summers. She loves Skiffington, that wooden, many-gabled, rambling building with its own private beach. It whispers of money, but in a reserved and dignified manner. As Court continues to explain the intricacies of mast and sail, Monica watches the red well-formed lips and wonders when he will kiss her again. Except for the Dubrovnik boy, who was probably nine when Monica knew him, Courtney is her first boyfriend.

"Where's your family?"

"In the cafeteria, drinking the embalming fluid they call coffee. And stashing away doughnuts. If the ferry sinks, you'll know why."

His eyes twinkle and she recognizes his style—a put-down of sorts in an English prep-school accent that fits a certain kind of humor that overstates or wryly understates everything. Few people can get away with it, but Courtney is subtle enough to manage it very well. It's a kind of banter her family would find foreign, yet she likes it.

"Do you think you'll be able to tear yourself away from the boat to get to the Festival?" Monica asks.

"Briefly. The boat comes first, you know," he says sadly, then snaps his fingers. "Say, what is all this about the Josef Kroll Trio concert? Is that your father?"

She nods.

"Just think, all that culture here in Genessee! We're planning to go. Monica . . ." He stops, somewhat embarrassed, then continues in a hesitant tone. "What do you think it will be like, seeing your father again?"

"Wonderful. It will be wonderful."

"Sure, of course. But aren't you just a little afraid? You haven't seen him for a long time, have you?"

She flushes, surprised that Courtney of all people should have fingered a fear she hardly dares face. So she flares up. "He is my father, after all. We . . . it isn't as if he were a stranger."

"You're right," Courtney assures her. Monica has noticed that he has always shied away from discussions of personal relationships. His parents seem to be so comfortably married that the very thought of divorce is unthinkable for him. It was only last summer that he confided to Monica that life without Mom and Dad, big sister Doris, and even his younger brother, Cyril, that bugger, who is away at an eastern school, would be painful to imagine.

"It's a long time since I've seen you, Monica. Let's go out on deck where we can say hello without everyone listening in on us."

She begins to follow him, but then a familiar voice is heard over the buzz of the crowd. The exaggerated English accent identifies it immediately as Courtney's mother.

"Oh there you are, Court! We've been searching for you everywhere. And Monica! Hello, my dear, so good to see you!"

She makes her way down the aisle with a hundred "Pardon me's" as she trips over the legs of the holiday crowd who are still sitting on the floor; her daughter,

Doris, two years older than Courtney, sulkily follows her.

Mrs. Phillips was born in England, and though she has lived in Canada for many years, she sees to it that her accent becomes more British with every passing season. The beauty-parlor waves of her dark hair, the well-tailored tweed skirt, and the bag of knitting that she carries suggest that she is playing the role of a well-bred English wife and mother. It is a pity that at the moment she is arguing with Doris about money, something about five dollars she lent her last week and ten the week before . . .

"Oh Motherrrr," Doris sighs. Monica is on her side. (In Irina's house, if you need money, you use it—if it can be found. "There could be a few dollars in the Hungarian cookbook, or if there's nothing there, I think I left five dollars in the cereal box under the oat flakes." Irina stashes bits of money all over the house; occasionally it all disappears. "It's the nature of money," she says.)

Mrs. Phillips breaks off the argument to chat with Monica, and then Mr. Phillips joins the group with a hearty Canadian "Good afternoon" to Monica. Before they can talk about the Festival, the ferry begins to dock, banging against the sides of the slip. An official voice blares out of the loudspeakers, but not a word can be understood.

"Hadn't we better get below quickly?" Mrs. Phillips asks.

"At the rate we're landing, I suggest a few games of cribbage," Court says.

"Oh, you!" His mother pushes him playfully, but her eyes are full of admiration.

Courtney insists on carrying Monica's canvas bag and book bag down below, though he complains that she has taken the whole library. A flurry of excitement grows as the passengers make their way to the car deck. Halfway down the narrow stairs, Mrs. Phillips stops and turns to Monica.

"Monica, will you have dinner with us tomorrow night?"

"Thanks, Mrs. Phillips, but I can't on Saturday. The concert, you know . . ."

"Of course! What am I thinking! How about Sunday night, then? Sixish."

"Come over in the afternoon so you can see the boat," Courtney begs.

"Hey, you're holding us up," the passengers behind them call impatiently. They apologize and move on quickly. Monica says thanks, she would love to come on Sunday.

"May I drive you home?" Mr. Phillips asks, for she lives nearly three miles from the ferry landing, but she says no thanks, her mother will be coming for her. So they get into their Rover and she waits with the foot passengers for the ferry to dock.

In less than a day now she will be seeing her father, perhaps here where the ferry is landing. The thought of it sets her heart beating fast again and drives the blood to her cheeks.

PART TWO

Bittersweet Place

────1

Here I Am!

At last the ferry comes to rest against the worn pilings. The chains are drawn back and gulls peer down on Monica and the other foot passengers, who march onto the island under the arched sign with its unpainted letters that spell GENESSEE ISLAND.

And where is her mother? Monica's eyes comb the waiting crowd but she does not see Irina, who always waits for her with Gabrielle jumping up and down in excitement and yelling "Yoo-hoo, Monica, here we are!" It is always a good reunion with lots of hugging and kissing and talking all at once as they walk to the car.

It is a terrible car, and every time Monica sees it, she realizes it is even worse than she remembered. They joke about The Maroon Ruin (although most of the maroon paint has been rubbed off) and they have long since decided that it hates people. The doors don't want to open, the hinges threaten to break apart, and yet once the doors are pried open they refuse to close. Torn upholstery. Periodically Irina has a "feeling" that next year they will have a new car, but it has not happened yet. This car has contributed to Monica's determination to marry a rich man.

Still, she would give anything to see it now. No car. No mother. No Gabrielle. The cars from the ferry stream homeward and the Phillipses wave to her as they pass by in their hearty Rover.

Monica picks up her carryall and curses herself for having brought home so many books. Damn and double damn! Still, she is not so much angry as hurt that on this most important weekend Irina has not come to meet her.

March on! She has no sooner begun the three-mile trek home when a familiar car, a neat gray Peugeot, overtakes her and stops.

"Jim Weed! It's so good to see you!" she cries.

"Good to see you too, Monica! I was afraid I'd missed you. Your mother asked me to pick you up."

"Where is she? She's all right, isn't she?" Monica asks, suddenly fearful.

"She's fine, terribly sorry she couldn't meet you herself, but Mrs. Heatherington called a last-minute Festival meeting and Irina couldn't get away from it. So I said I'd leave the hospital lab on my coffee break and pick you up. Do get in. These all your bags?"

"Jim, you are so nice! I appreciate this. You'll never know how I dreaded walking home with this load."

"Well, I'm always glad to help your mother, especially when she's so busy."

"What's she so busy about?" Monica asks. Now that she knows Irina is all right, she pouts like an unreasonable child, hurt because her mother hasn't defied Mrs. Heatherington to come and meet her.

"There's the Festival," Jim says in his slow even tones, "and of course there's the shop, and just this week she decided to repaint the bathroom and bedrooms, in case she has guests this weekend."

Oh-ho-ho, Monica says to herself, so she expects guests!

"Why does she always have to wait until the last minute and then tackle everything?" she asks Jim. It's a rhetorical question, for this is exactly what one would expect of Irina.

"I was hoping to help her," Jim says. What a sweet man he is, Monica thinks, and what a shame that he is never taken seriously. Somewhere he has nine sisters, no brothers, and his parents were cruel enough to name him Jimson Weed, as though he were not wanted. Monica applauds this gentle man for having changed his name to James or Jim. Yet he does resemble a weed, a long plant reaching for the sun. Long thin legs, a long thin body, and white skin that never tans. It is obvious that he is in love with Irina, which is why he is happy to do so many things for her, even offer to help paint the guest room, knowing he will never be a guest there himself. For Irina, who has a magical way of attracting people to her, does not appear to be in love with anyone. In fact, she continues to refer to Josef almost as though they were still married.

"How is school? Lots of work, I'll bet, with exams coming up."

"It's murderous. I've even got to do a paper over vacation."

"Your mother's very proud of you and of that school. She's counting on your getting a scholarship again."

Monica frowns; this is not Jim's problem, but hers, and possibly her mother's. Kindness does not admit him to the family. Yet it is silly to be upset with him, for there is nothing but gentleness about him as he drives over the blue macadam road through the familiar Island landscape, melancholy on this sunless afternoon.

"There's something I think you should know, Monica. Do you mind if we stop to talk for a minute or so?"

"My mother's not having another crisis, is she?" Monica asks, wanting to cover her ears and not hear another word about Irina's crises, Irina's failures.

"Part of your mother's charm is that she's never bogged down. Remarkable survival powers," Jim says as he parks the car at a scene-viewing place; but there is no scene to view, only the thickening fog, which makes Monica feel suddenly trapped and isolated.

"Your mother doesn't want to upset you so she won't tell you everything. Still, you ought to know. I'm afraid the shop will close down. It's a shame, that nice little place she's made, but it isn't even earning enough to pay its rent. Genessee isn't big enough yet for a wool shop."

"It should do very well through the summer with all the summer people here, shouldn't it?"

"Maybe. I think perhaps I can help her with the rent through July, anyway. And then we can see."

"Jim, you are too good; I wonder if you should. Can't the Arts Council take it over, or the Artists' Co-op?"

"No money there either. The good artists, like Kathryn, sell on the mainland."

"It was such a dumb idea to begin with. 'Irina's Knittery'!" Monica says, not hiding her exasperation. Her mother has put all her capital—i.e., the divorce settlement and a few family jewels she has sold—into this shop, which is indeed charming with its small Franklin stove, the tea that is offered to visitors whether they buy anything or not, and her mother crocheting all the while and helping others. In the beginning, it had seemed as if the Island people were dying for a place like this where they could buy wools for knitting and crocheting, and needlepoint supplies, and where the work of island craftsmen could be displayed with Irina's shawls and sweaters, which are now and then unexpectedly beautiful.

"Poor Mother!" Monica says in the next breath. "She tries so hard! But she still has a ballet class and she teaches in the schools, doesn't she?"

"She's a wonder—teaches dancing, folksinging, even knitting. Kids love her. But she's only an auxiliary teacher because she doesn't have any credentials—"

"Doesn't even have a high-school diploma," Monica interrupts.

"And so she gets minimum wage, and it's truly minimal. With summer coming, that will end."

"So that's it!" Monica says. "Thanks for telling me, Jim. I plan to get a real job this summer, maybe waiting on tables, so that will help."

Brave words, and yet her voice has taken on a nervous tremor that means she doesn't know how they will manage. An image comes back . . . the night that Irina drove north and would not turn back. But that's over and done with. If Josef should by any chance take Monica home with him, which of course is what she prays for, then she will see to it that he sends money home to Irina and Gabrielle.

"I sure hate to start your weekend with bad news. Strictly confidential, all right? What really keeps your mother's spirits up is the fact that you go to that good school."

"And the Festival keeps her going too, I'll bet,"

Monica says as Jim backs out of the scenic spot and drives homeward. "By the way, what ever happened to that billboard she painted, the one advertising the Festival? She sent me a sketch of it—the one with the rainbow over Genessee."

Jim shakes his head.

"Something went wrong? I know. It had to happen."

"It was a beautiful, fine, lyrical painting that she did. Everyone loved it. Only she used the wrong kind of paint. For three days it glowed, and then we had a storm and the rainbow dripped down, and all the letters dripped down; it looked as if Genessee and the rainbow were sinking into the ocean. So they had to replace it!"

"Poor Mama! It's just her luck," Monica says sympathetically, and yet it is rather funny in a way she cannot explain, and she begins to laugh. Jim smiles, his even teeth gleaming white.

"That's true. The things that happen to your mother just couldn't happen to anyone else. And yet she has so much spirit. An admirable woman in every way!"

It is a good thing they have arrived at the cottage, or he would spend the rest of the afternoon praising Irina. He stops in front of the wooden gate.

"Thanks for everything, Jim—the ride and for telling me about my mother. Well, I guess we'll be seeing you."

"I'll be over tonight, to see if I can help in any way," Jim says. He nods good-bye and drives off.

Monica stands in front of the yellow wooden house with its lilac bushes, blooming miracles of lavender and white fragrance. Louka, the cat, sits on the rail of the verandah, her fat sides neatly balanced over each edge. She blinks at Monica. The sign over the porch is more faded than ever, yet Monica says the words out loud: "Bittersweet Place."

What name could be more appropriate! Monica shakes her head, then picks up her bags and walks up the steps.

_____2

Bittersweet

"Hello? Hello? Hello? Hey, I'm home!"

Her voice echoes. The house is silent, empty. She knows that Irina is at a meeting but calls anyway. At least Gabrielle could have waited for her, but her sister seems to be away from home most of the time now, playing with her friends—Rosemary or Valerie or Cynthia. She thrives on other people, moves in and out of her friends' homes without hesitation. Only Louka follows Monica inside and rubs against her leg. Two kittens jump out from under the sofa and try to nurse Louka, who shrugs them off impatiently.

This cottage, so ordinary when they first came, has in some mysterious way become her mother's house, as though it were a masterpiece with the bold signature IRINA blazing on it. It is filled with things, hundreds of things: hand-turned pots ranging in size from tiny vases to enormous bulbous jars, many sprouting dried weeds; pillows everywhere, pillows woven, block-printed,

batiked, and embroidered in a myriad of colors and
shapes; baskets, boxes, shells, amber worry beads, Es-
kimo sculptures, a guitar, a papier-mâché dragon that
Gabrielle made in second grade; and numerous paintings, among them one of Irina as a young ballet dancer
in a white tutu and an enormous pseudo-Matisse that
dates from the period when Irina thought she would
become a painter. The knitted and crocheted things that
Irina will display at her booth at the Festival the next
day cover the red velvet sofa, the chairs and coffee
tables: shawls, sweaters, caps, booties, afghans, and
long skirts. The room pulsates with color. After the
sterile atmosphere of Chatham, this room is dizzying in
its gypsy wildness.

And how does Irina manage to collect so much when
she has no money? It is a kind of genius that enables
her to find treasures in the city dump, or to trade a
sweater for a piece of sculpture or that handsome
stained-glass window made by an island artisan. "You
don't need money, only a desire to have something," is
her philosophy, "and so you find a way!" She is given
gifts, and yet she gives of herself freely too; she finds
things; she trades; and more often than not, if she can
get it in no other way, she will *make* what she wants.

And yet summer is on the way and there will be no
money coming in. What then?

Monica sits at the upright piano, plays a chord, and
notices that her mother has at last had the piano tuned.
For Gabrielle? But Gabrielle hardly cares. Monica
plays what she remembers of a Bach prelude, but her
fingers are stiff. Halfway through she stumbles, re-
trieves the theme, but loses it again. Her fingers will not
obey. Now the tears come, ridiculous tears, a quick sob

and a burst of anger as she beats the piano with her fist—and immediately apologizes with a soft conciliatory chord.

"My fault. It's my own dumb fault," she tells Louka, who stares at her with green grape eyes. "I could have taken lessons at Chatham, but I don't know . . ." Louka doesn't understand, nor does she. When she first arrived at school, she played better than any other girl there, yet when she sat down at the grand piano to play, there seemed to be no reason for her to practice.

It was the last of many pianos in her life.

It was her father who insisted that there be pianos wherever they stayed on long concert tours, and what instruments they were! Old square pianos with sculptured legs, grand pianos ten feet long, tiny clavichords sometimes painted with cherubs and flowers, stern uprights, and, in Paris, a jazzy black lacquered piano.

For La Californie he bought a baby grand piano and asked the great Mr. Bernardi to teach her. Nervously she performed for him while he stood behind her and smoked a cigar. He did not proclaim her a genius, but nodded and promised that with infinite work and patience she would someday play well.

The hours of practice, those long lonely hours of "infinite work and patience" that she gave to that piano! And without complaining, for she would have it no other way. One day she would accompany her father as he played; it was all she asked. She even studied accompaniments to violin pieces and had dared to begin the beloved Franck

Sonata in A major, difficult as it was. Someday, she believed, she would master it . . .

And then there was that April night when her mother shook her from a deep sleep and told her to hurry. And the night of the piano recital when she would have performed a Beethoven sonata passed while she mourned in Canada.

It was then that something ended; a black curtain fell over the keyboard.

More autobiography? But can she actually put that in? Probably not.

"Enough!" she cries, and jumps from the piano stool to race upstairs, where it smells of paint. She tears off her uniform in the small bedroom she shares with Gabrielle. As usual, there is about it a seaside dampness and chill, yet she is fond of it for a certain country quaintness, the braided rug and, under the sloping eaves, the two narrow beds—Gabrielle's covered with dozens of dolls, stuffed animals, and a long pillow made to resemble a snake. Her own bed is covered with a chaste white old-fashioned spread and its only ornament is another of Louka's kittens.

Monica finds a pair of old jeans, a sweater, and the white woolen poncho with an intricate blue border that Irina once made for her. Even though Irina's fingers fly as she works, it took hours to make this wrap that Monica now throws on so casually.

She stands still for nearly a minute alternating between love and hate, for she loves the silence of the house; at Chatham, there was always noise; one could never be alone there. Yet she hates an empty house. The truth is that she misses her mother's spirited greeting, that delightful babble of English and French with a few Hungarian endearments, and the long graceful arms holding her in a loving hug.

Then she turns and runs downstairs and out of the house. She must see somebody! Aunt Kathryn, then.

_____3

Visit with a Surrogate Aunt

As she strides along the narrow road and up to Kathryn's, Monica wonders if she should mention her relatives in the autobiography. Miss Cornwall has emphasized the importance of one's family.

What family, what relatives? She recalls herself as a flower girl at a wedding where she was adored, picked up, and fondled by a throng of aunts, uncles, cousins, and grandparents as well as great-aunts and -uncles. And later all of them clapping their hands and beating their toes in time to the music as her father and mother danced by themselves on the dance floor.

She remembers a particularly nasty cousin, a small boy who poured ice cubes down her back. And a jewel of a memory, a great-grandmother, a tiny, tiny lady dressed in black, ears pierced with tiny gold earrings and eyes for nobody but "her little Josef," who towered above her. She poured tea from a silver pot and pressed thin buttery wafers into Monica's hands. She spoke Hungarian, French, and a little Russian, but hardly any English. A week after the tea party she died.

As for her mother's side—"Forget it!" Irina advised. "We meet at funerals and that's enough. They're full of vinegar, all of them."

Monica longed for a family like those in children's books: closely knit sisters and big brothers to protect her, fun-loving cousins, kindly aunts, and gruff fascinating uncles who would give her silver dollars now and then.

"If only I had someone, a cousin or an aunt, someone who was always there," she complained to Irina, who answered tartly:

"Always there whether you want them or not! Be grateful you're free of all that." She too had inherited a touch of the family vinegar.

But Aunt Kathryn is a stroke of the best kind of luck. Because she is not really family, she enjoys a certain detachment and is free of the stormy temperament of Josef's family and the "vinegar" of Irina's. Unlike them, she is always there.

And now that Monica has pulled the Swiss cowbell that hangs on the door of the cottage, Kathryn appears, tall and lanky. Is she old or not? Impossible to be sure with that fine bony face and the gray hair that is pulled back and held with a Chinese ornament of straw and allowed to fall freely as though she were seventeen. Irina estimates that she is seventy, Gabrielle guesses thirty-six and seven months, and Monica can only assume that somewhere in between lies the truth.

"Monica! I was hoping you'd come today, and here you are! Come in!"

She actually kisses Monica's cheek without blowing into the air as women frequently do when greeting one another. Then she steps back to study her young friend.

"Let me feast my eyes! You're blooming. Take off those hideous glasses and let me see your eyes. Ah, Monica, you're going to be a smoldering beauty, believe me, with that reserved exterior and all the fire banked inside!"

Monica laughs at the extravagant praise.

"You're the one who looks marvelous," she says, but it is not entirely true, for she sees circles under Kathryn's eyes and suspects she is not as well as she could be. "I've wanted to talk with you so many times, Kathryn."

"Same here. So come in and talk with me now. But let's close the door. Imagine, this chill in May . . . brrrr. I'll put up some tea and then I want you to tell me everything about you and school and that infamous Midnight Club."

Monica follows her to the tiny kitchen, where two canaries in a bamboo cage that rises like a pagoda make such a sweet loud chatter that Kathryn scolds them: "*Tais-toi*, how can I talk with Monica when you make such a racket?"

"How are the pots and the new sculptures?" Monica asks Kathryn as she brews the tea in a pot of her own making.

"Without any modesty, I shall tell you, my dear, that they are doing very well. I sent off a large shipment of pots to Vancouver yesterday, one of my bowls made an enormous prestigious craft exhibition, and I'll be having a one-person show in Seattle this fall. There's even an article about me in a magazine, can you imagine, although it's not too significant. Still, it means I can manage payments on the studio and keep the canaries in birdseed and myself in tea. What else can anyone possibly want?"

A fabulous woman, Monica thinks. She has lost three husbands one way or another—that is, by divorce from the first, the death of the second, and desertion by the third, who took most of her savings with him. Her children have long since grown up and scattered, and they visit only rarely. Yet she does not complain. Can she be well? Her head shakes a little as she talks—a tremor so slight it is barely perceptible, a kind of perpetual motion. Monica wants to ask, but will not, of course. Kathryn disregards the tremor, takes another sip of hot cinnamon tea, and puts an arm around Monica's shoulders.

"Let's sit in the living room now and hear about *you*. You're the one with the exciting life."

"Exciting! Hardly that."

"Come now, I thought you adored it."

"Well, some of that is window dressing. I guess I do like it; at least I'm grateful. The first year it was like pretending to be at an English boarding school out of some novel. But now it seems just too unreal, a rich girls' school. I miss meeting all kinds of people, the way it was at Berkeley. And it's not easy being a poor mouse among the rich girls."

"I'm surprised to hear you talk like this. It takes more than money to be good in English or math or hockey or anything. And the standards there are high for everyone, rich or poor, aren't they?"

"Of course. Classes are fine, impersonal but disci-
plined. I never thought I'd be grateful for that, yet there
it is! Perhaps I can say it another way. Hardly anybody
wants to recognize the real problems of today. They'd
be happier if we were still in the nineteenth century."

"But there's your Midnight Club. You're talking with
girls who are living now. They can't all have nineteenth-
century problems, can they?"

"Not in the least. They're very human; I like them, I
really do, even if some of them are very '*rich* human'—
as if they had fences around them so they can't really
see a world bigger than their own lives. And then there
are silly things, like chapel."

"Oh, chapel! I remember it well. The school I went
to was very much like yours, only on the East Coast.
Chapel seemed outmoded. Yet sometimes now when
I'm turning out pots or shaping a bowl, I find myself
singing a tune and it often turns out to be something I
learned in chapel. I'm not the kind of believer who goes
around singing hymns, and yet I find something very
foursquare, solid, and comforting about them. It's odd I
should remember them when I suspect I've forgotten
just about everything else."

Monica smiles politely though she cannot see herself
ever singing hymns. She had not intended for the conversation to go this way at all. Kathryn is watching her
closely; she puts down her teacup and gazes directly into
her eyes.

"Monica, my dear, do you know I have the feeling
that you are skirting all around the edge of something,
and that chapel and the rich girls and the nineteenth-
century aspect are not really what you're talking about?
H'm? What is it?"

Monica has told nobody her plans, not a soul, but she must tell someone. Only Kathryn can be trusted. She breathes deeply, then blurts out the truth in a dramatic whisper.

"I want to finish school in Berkeley; I want my father to take me back and let me live with him there."

"Oh you do, do you? Does he know about this?"

"No. But I've been dreaming of this for a long time now. We were torn apart, and I want to heal that break before I go off to college, because by then it will be too late. And maybe, possibly, I'll be able to get back to my piano. And life is so much bigger and fuller in Berkeley. At least it seems real."

"And what about your mother?"

"I wouldn't want her to be hurt, but even she can see that originally I had *two* parents. I can't just throw my father away."

"But has he tried to get you back? Perhaps I don't understand . . ."

"Well, Kathryn . . ." Monica's voice falters dangerously and she stands up, looks through a window, and pretends to be studying a bush full of white blooms. The reserve she has practiced at school helps considerably, and she is able to steady her voice.

"Why is my father coming here to give a concert? He doesn't need engagements; his trio is doing well. And Genessee is out of the way. He divorced Irina, so it stands to reason he is coming here basically to see his children. He never knew Gabrielle very well, but he and I were very close."

She rests her case, but Kathryn speaks with eyes averted.

"Dear child, your father is being paid handsomely

for this concert, for one thing, so it's well worth his while to come here. Besides, on Sunday night he has an engagement in Seattle, so this is not a great out-of-the-way trip after all."

What can Monica say after this? Kathryn gets up, puts a gentle hand on her shoulder, and comforts her as best she can. "We're both in the dark about this, Monica. You may be right. I don't want to worry you, but I have a weakness for facts. You understand?"

Monica knows that facts can wear different faces so she does not argue with Kathryn, who is only trying to save her from possible defeat. But she doesn't intend to be defeated, so she changes the subject.

"My mother writes that you are doing magnificent new things. Can you let me peek at them, Kathryn? Mother raves so about them."

"She should be my agent. Irina can describe a garbage can so it sounds like a work of art. Anyway, come ahead!"

The studio is large and professionally designed compared to the cozy intimacy of the cottage. Kathryn and her favorite husband constructed the studio from an old barn, making a cement floor, moving walls, building shelves, and setting up a workshop. Long rows of vases and pots are lined up waiting for their final glazes, each one serene and perfectly molded, no two alike.

"Those are for the shops," Kathryn says, "and these are new. Experimental. This piece here, for example."

She shows Monica a large coiled planter that is subtly curved; a pattern of roots seems to emerge through the jade-green glaze. The vases, urns, and bird-baths are highly sculptural, yet they bloom with unexpected flowerings of red, purple, and blue glaze. And at the far end of the studio Kathryn shows Monica her "playthings," ceramic sculptures of birds, animals, heads, and figures of people, all fantastically colored and molded, like objects seen in a dream or under water.

"They're marvelous! Different from what you've done," Monica says. It is not easy to express how she feels about works of art, but Kathryn must sense how moved she is.

"It's a new direction, I suppose. Every piece I do is like the very first. One begins again and again and again and again. And always in a slightly new direction, going further than you went before."

Is this why she seems so ageless, so timeless? Because she has no fears and looks ahead instead of clutching to the past, refusing to reproduce *ad infinitum* only those safe conventional pots? Monica senses something in this that relates to her, but she cannot quite grasp it as yet.

"I wish I could do this, even turn out one simple pot," she says.

"If you're around this summer, be my guest. I have an extra wheel, and we can work together."

"Oh Kathryn, would you let me, really?" Forgetting her newly acquired reserve, Monica hugs her, seeing herself in this new role, turning out rows of subtly curved pots and jars. Then she remembers she may be back in California. "That is, if I'm still around here this summer."

"Naturally," Kathryn says, now leading her out the back door to the garden. "Summer's not for a while yet. By the way, would you be a darling and take back some fresh herbs to your mother?"

She takes a garden knife from her pocket and moves

slowly to her knees, as though her joints are stiff. She shoos away a chicken that has wandered into her garden, then selects a choice bouquet of parsley, thyme, chives, and a sprig of rosemary. She chatters about putting in a new cold frame.

"What do you suppose your mother will do once you've gone back to California with your father?"

Monica frowns. This worries her, particularly since her conversation with Jim Weed. "I just don't know."

"She'll miss you, Monica, and she'll feel sorry if you don't finish at Chatham. Of course your mother has many friends here, and I believe she loves the Island, no matter what she says. But it's not easy . . ." Kathryn's voice drifts off, as though she doesn't want to finish the sentence.

As they return to the kitchen, where Kathryn will wrap the herbs in a sheet of newspaper, she remarks, "Something came through the mail that might interest your mother. A letter from a friend of mine in Seattle. She runs a travel agency and will need an assistant in the fall, and asked if I knew of anyone. I'm not sure whether Irina would be interested or not, but you might ask her."

"You can't be serious!" Monica laughs, seeing her mother arranging tours for thousands of tourists who wish to go to Paris or Rome but instead find themselves stranded in Reykjavik or Tunis or Afghanistan and other places they never intended to visit, because when her mother arranges things that is how they turn out—disastrous.

"I'll tell her," Monica promises. "And thank you so much, Kathryn. Every time I see you, I feel so very much better."

"What a nice thing to say! I love you too. And I

might see you tonight, just might drop in at Bittersweet Place, but it's not exactly a promise. So long, Monica! Thanks for coming."

Happier now (is it the tea? Kathryn? remembering that her father is coming home tomorrow?), she runs home. Her mother, who has seen her from the bedroom window, rushes down the stairs and into the street to greet her daughter. Laughing, she hugs her, murmuring how good it is to see Monica again.

"She is really very young," Monica realizes; she has never considered her mother in just that way before, "almost like a girl."

4

Home Again

It has begun to rain gently. Inside it is warm. Home. Monica sits in the familiar kitchen, legs propped up on a chair as she eats a slice of bread that Irina has spread thickly with fresh butter. Nobody in the world can make bread like her mother, and the butter that comes from the churn of a local farmwife is like no other butter she has ever had. Louka sleeps on the kitchen table; Irina is perhaps the only mother in the world who does not get hysterical at the sight of a cat on the table. Irina stands at the stove stirring Kathryn's herbs into the bouillabaisse, and the familiar tantalizing odors fill the kitchen. That fragrance is so good, so nostalgic . . .

> *Again Monica is a child and this is the summer the Krolls spent on the outskirts of Nice in southern France. Her mother made bouillabaisse all the time, so it seemed. Brilliant image of herself, eight years old, coming home from the market with her mother, who carries a basket full of fish, crayfish, lobster, shrimp, and whatever else she has found, each new item a treasure, this particular lemon and that particular bunch of parsley, and of course they* must *get those shallots. Monica is allowed to carry the long crusty loaves of bread in a blue string bag. Irina wears a wide-brimmed straw hat and a full skirt, and could be a costumed character out of a light opera. Tourists notice her, ask if they may take her picture.*
>
> *At the villa she bursts into song: "Here I am! Here I am! Here I am!" She sings joyfully and loudly but sharp, at least half a tone sharp, and Josef covers his ears as though pained. Irina sings nevertheless, bends over to soothe him with a kiss. She moves, with the grace of a ballet dancer.*

What a good mama, to be so alive and to make such magnificent soups, then and now, so that the kitchen becomes steamy, warm, and full of pungent odors while it becomes colder outside and it still rains.

Yet there are differences between then, when Mama sang so loudly as she stirred the soup, and now, when she frowns a little. Then Irina had enough money so that she could choose the best of ingredients. Now the bouillabaisse is made with the clams her mother has probably dug that very morning at the beach. Fish heads bob in the broth, giving flavor to the soup. What other treasures the soup contains are the last of an exchange Irina has made with the local fish dealer. She "styles" and cuts his hair in exchange for so much fish. "If only the butcher would do this too, we'd get by," Irina has remarked more than once, but the butcher is bald. And so they eat fish.

In short, they are poor. Still, they exist.

Irina chatters about everything but the big event. "How is school? How is Sheila? Are you on the tennis team this term? And did you see Courtney on the ferry? I heard the family was coming down."

She moves through the kitchen with the lightness of a dancer. Monica puts down the bread and butter. "Oh Mother, how easy it is for you to be slender! I have to work so hard to lose a few pounds."

"Don't be silly. You are beautiful, or you would be if only it weren't for those awful glasses. Never mind, we'll get you contacts one of these days! As for me, I'm all skin and bones," she says deprecatingly, but with a touch of pride. "Go ahead, eat it, they don't have good bread like that at school, do they?"

"Not in the least," Monica says, but she feeds the rest of the slice to Louka, who will eat anything. An insatiable cat. Monica knows that her father likes slender women, and so she has gone without desserts for three weeks now. She is determined to be thin, whatever the cost.

Monica wants to ask about the weekend—so many questions must be answered—but Gabrielle bursts through the door and rushes to hug and kiss Monica as though they had been separated for the last five years. Gabrielle, now nine years old, moves lightly, and for a moment Monica has the impression that she is seeing her mother as a child.

"We've been *dying* to see you," she says, although she must have known Monica would have been home for at least three hours by now. She did not want to leave her friends. "I can understand that," Monica thinks, but she feels hurt all the same.

Suddenly Gabrielle breaks off the affectionate embrace and stands in exasperation, hand on one hip, ready to complain of something. In spite of the chilly weather, she wears thin cotton shorts, summer socks, and a light T-shirt that says WHAM, BANG, WHIZ, SPLAT!

"Mama, I can't put flowers on my hat for the hat contest tomorrow, like you said I should, because *Valerie* is wearing flowers on *her* hat."

"What difference does that make?" Irina asks, as she places soup bowls in the oven to warm.

"Mo-thurrrrr, we can't *both* have flowers on our hats. That's copying, and Valerie thought of it first and she's my *best friend*."

"You could use vegetables. They can be beautiful," Monica suggests. "Do you have a hat to put them on?"

Gabrielle rummages around the back verandah and returns with a basket upside down on her head. It is too large and slips down over her eyes. "Just this dumb thing. Valerie has a *real* hat that belonged to her grandmother."

"Monica's right," her mother says, "what's wrong with vegetables? Beautiful colors and shapes! A stalk of celery, a few banana peels, onion skins—which are gorgeous—orange peel. Fantastic!"

"But Mama, that's *garbage!*" Gabrielle cries.

"Do you want to win the prize or not?" Irina asks realistically. "Then listen. The judges want something original." But her mind is really on the bouillabaisse, which still doesn't measure up to her standards. "It's the saffron that's missing, of course. Saffron," she sighs. "Too expensive. Oh, what I would do for a pinch of saffron!"

Monica understands that Gabrielle is worried about the hat. "It doesn't have to look like garbage at all, honey. We can use that curly stuff, kale; Kathryn has some in her garden. A few red radishes, a sprig of broccoli—which is really a flower. I'll help you."

Still Gabrielle pouts. "I s'pose I could put a cup of salad dressing on top and let it spill over as I parade around."

Irina pretends not to notice the sarcasm. "Now that's an *original* idea. The judges will love it."

Monica sets the table, lights a candle in a Chianti bottle, and carries over the pot of soup from the stove. Everything bears such a sweet familiarity—the chipped blue enamel dipper and the red embroidered linen cloth, now mended and worn, and the three of them sitting around the table together. Louka purrs in her lap. This *is* home, then, and this scene will flash before her eyes long after she has left the Island, when she will dream of home. But this is too difficult to express, so she praises the soup.

"At school, no matter what they cook, it comes out like white sauce, bland and blah."

"Like baby throw-up, I bet," Gabrielle says. "Ugh, I wouldn't want to go there."

"But the school is wonderful anyway, really exciting,

in spite of the food," Monica says, just as though she hadn't complained of it that very afternoon to Kathryn. "Maybe you'll go there sometime, Gabrielle."

Her sister makes a face and a disgusting noise. "I don't want to leave the Island."

But you *should*, Monica is thinking; there's a time when one has to leave. Gabrielle will not discuss it; instead she chats about the ponies that will be parading at the Festival and makes Monica promise that she will watch her dance in the Butterfly Ballet. Irina talks about the booth she will have and Monica is thinking how splendid it is to anticipate this happy day, each of them glowing with it, when the telephone rings. Gabrielle jumps up to answer it.

"Mama," she calls, "Cynthia wants me to have dinner and stay over at her house tomorrow night. Can I?"

"Your father's coming. There's the concert. Tell Cynthia some other time."

"All *right*," Gabrielle says gracelessly.

Yet no sooner does she sit down when the telephone rings again, and then again and still again. Each time Gabrielle jumps up. The holiness of the meal—if that is not too strong an expression—is broken.

"Mother, she needs to be taught some manners. You never used to let me talk over the phone during meals. Gabrielle needs discipline."

"Now, Monica, she's only a child."

But before Monica can say any more about it, Irina herself is called to the phone to discuss a detail of the Festival, and only three minutes later an irate customer phones to complain that the needlepoint yarn she ordered has not yet come in and she might as well go to

Victoria for it as wait for it here. Irina soothes her, then returns to the soup, which has now grown cold. Gabrielle has left the table and returns with a canvas flight bag packed with nightgown and toothbrush.

"Where do you think you're going?"

"I'm gonna sleep at Rosemary's tonight. I told you, Mama."

"That's right, you did. Wait a minute. What about practicing?"

"Okay," Gabrielle says, "but only fifteen minutes because it's a holiday."

While Monica and her mother drink coffee, Gabrielle practices the piano. She plays beginner pieces, stammering through them with errors, and it is clear she does not care whether she plays well or not. At her age, Monica recalls, she had studied all the Bartók Microcosmos, a number of Scarlatti sonatas, and had already performed a Beethoven sonata. Who teaches Gabrielle that she cares so little for music?

"Mother, can't you find a good teacher? This is just a waste, and you just can't waste time. First lessons are so important."

"Try to find a good teacher on the Island! Anyway, Monica, we may not be here much longer." She smiles knowingly, as if she has a secret. "Does she," Monica wonders, "and would she confide in Monica?"

"Can I go now? Have I practiced enough?" Gabrielle calls out.

"Yes, darling. Be back early tomorrow morning, though," Irina answers.

She resembles a sprite in the yellow raincoat and sou'wester hat, a Goodwill bargain, and she chatters, embraces her mother and sister, and says if only Rosemary didn't expect her, she'd be so glad to stay home. Then she skips out the door.

"Mama, why does she leave home all the time? Why do you let her go so much?" Monica asks, vaguely worried for her younger sister. Irina remains calm, smiles archly over her cup of coffee, and assures Monica:

"Gabrielle will be all right. And now that she's gone, you and I can have a little talk!"

5

Monica and Her Mother

Irina's eyes gleam as she refills Monica's coffee cup and her own. She does not seem so much like a mother now as a friend, a fellow conspirator. Monica isn't sure that she likes this equal footing, and nearly envies Gabrielle in her light-footed childhood.

"All right, Mother, come across. I recognize your fine hand in all this. What's the idea of getting Daddy up here for a concert?"

"*My* hand? *My* idea?" Irina says in mock surprise, as if she had nothing to do with the arrangements. "It's mostly the Pouter Pigeon's idea. Mrs. Heatherington heard that the Kroll Trio is becoming famous, and so why not begin with them on the Island's 'march to culture'? Yes, that's how she puts it!" The idea amuses

Irina. Her eyes are twinkling, she is so full of eagerness.

"And of course you didn't put that notion in her head?"

"Naturally not, but then I could hardly disagree."

"Mother, there are thousands of musicians, so why did you decide on him? You're *divorced*, Mother. Can't you face the fact?"

"Divorce is only a word. Your father and I belong to each other, really belong, no matter what those silly little pieces of legal paper say."

"But Mother, *you* left *him,* remember? What can you expect now?"

"Of course I remember what I did. Perhaps I went a little too far, but I have always known he would come up here after us. And see—he is coming."

"It's not the same thing," Monica insists. "He was asked."

"You were only a little girl then, so you wouldn't know what it's like to have a husband who carries on with other women . . . you are *still* too young to know about such things."

"Mother, I wasn't that little then, and certainly I understand now. Besides . . ." Monica cannot finish the sentence. The knot of resentment she has had for so long rises like a hard little knob to her throat and she can neither swallow it nor spit it out. If only her mother had not left Berkeley, it would have worked out so differently . . . But there is no room for "iffery." It is clear that Irina intends for Josef to take her back, and Monica cannot see him doing this. Yet Irina sees it as clearly as she, Monica, imagines that her father will take *her* back.

Irina lights a cigarette at the end of the long ivory

holder and breathes deeply. "Look at the facts, Monica. I've looked at them day after day after day. He has never remarried, and why? Obviously because nobody can satisfy him the way I can. When I think of that wonderfully gay, romantic, and often difficult life we led before we settled in Berkeley, the way we used to dance . . . ah, the way your father dances! And the crazy things we used to do! When you and Gabrielle were sleeping, we sometimes used to run down to the beach, take off all our clothes, and run in the moonlight . . ."

She dreams of all this, but Monica is appalled at the thought of her parents running along the beach in the buff. After all . . .

"And in Berkeley, other places too, he loved people, was always bringing people home. Do you remember, the musicians and composers and playwrights and heaven-knows-who, all kinds of marvelous, fascinating people? After concerts, unexpectedly for dinner, and of course at our famous Sunday morning brunches. And they *were* famous! Do you know why Josef always brought people home? Because he was proud of me, and of you and Gabrielle too."

"Mother, be realistic. Have you forgotten those awful fights you used to have when you threw dishes at each other and yelled so loud all the neighbors could hear? Do you think *I* could forget those scenes?"

"Don't take it so seriously, darling. A good fight is a way of clearing the air, that's all. And then you make up afterward. So sweet! But come with me. I've got things to show you. Come on, and smile, don't be so serious."

Irina opens the refrigerator and Monica blinks at the

abundance on the shelves: cheeses, olives, a riot of fruit in and out of season, and plastic bag after bag, each filled with a different kind of pastry.

"Mother, what's the idea? You must have been baking for a week. All this marvelous food!"

"It's for Sunday morning. Mrs. H. insists that the trio stay with her and I can argue with her only so much, but Josef is coming here to be with us Sunday morning. And then you will witness the beauty of reunion. A second marriage! You and Gabrielle will be maids of honor."

"Mother, you're out of your mind!"

"No, my darling, I've never been more sane. Couples divorce and remarry; it happens all the time. We belong together, Josef and I. He knows it and so do I. As God is my witness, I know this must be true."

And if Josef could see her as she is now, Monica believes, she could be right, for she is irresistible at that moment, seeming very young with her eyes glowing and her long tapering hands gesturing. Possibly it might work. Each will regret their mistakes and grow to love the other again for the rest of their lives, like that old couple on the ferry. And she and Gabrielle will live with them both. It is a magnificent dream!

"And now come upstairs and see the bedroom," Irina says, pulling her daughter after her.

"It's lovely," Monica says, praising the lavender bathroom and the delicate eggshell walls of the bedroom, the yellow trim. "But why do it now, at the last minute?"

"It simply occurred to me that we might have company," Irina says lightly; she does not elaborate, and Monica guesses that she is hoping Josef will be the guest. Monica can do nothing about her mother's dreams. Obediently she sits on the bed while Irina pulls from the wardrobe all the clothes she has been assembling for the weekend. She chatters as Monica sees another image.

Berkeley. She is ten years old, sitting in a drugstore behind a display of stockings, "stealing a read" in the comic books she would never have dared bring home, when she hears a familiar voice. Her mother is in the store! She wears a silky shirt and white jersey silky pants over her svelte elongated figure; a persimmon scarf is tied around her black hair. She is talking with two women, faculty wives, so drab and lumpish that Monica cannot help but feel her mother's superiority.

After Irina leaves, however, the two women chat.

"You know," one says, "I've never really figured out Irina Kroll. Tell me, is she very bright or is she very dumb?"

"I've been wondering that myself," the other woman cackles.

Nasty stinks, jealous old hags, Monica hisses after them. Yet as she lies awake in bed that night, she is bothered. Funny that they should worry whether Irina is smart or dumb. Monica has never even thought of it. What she has always worried about is whether her mother is beautiful or not.

"I've made this for Gabrielle. A little peasanty, but cute, don't you think so? And here's a blue shirt for you, Monica . . . I found a wool remnant . . ."

The odd thing about her mother is that she can be as dignified as a countess or duchess, Monica thinks. When she attends concerts with her black hair piled up in curls, wearing extravagant gowns and capes, long white kid gloves, and glittering jewels—earrings four inches long!—there is an air of excitement about her, and Monica has heard people whisper in admiration, "Who is she?"

But there is that other Irina too. It was hardly a week before the scene in the drugstore that Monica bumped into her unexpectedly one rainy afternoon. She had been to a rummage sale, wore a hideous green raincoat, a faded kerchief over her hair, and flappy boots, though there was no need for her to appear so ragged. Worse yet was her face, pale, without makeup, and the eyes large and tragic; a nightmare of poverty that Monica could not shake from her mind, even though Irina, well dressed at dinner that night and gaily chattering, was handsome Irina again.

Poverty is ugly, Monica thinks. And she cannot prevent the image of a visit to a Brooklyn street where Irina grew up and where her mother still lived. She will never forget the garbage-strewn streets, an old woman stumbling past, and the jeering voices of children playing behind ash cans and pretending to kill her as she clung to her mother.

"And now the *pièce de résistance*!" Irina says, taking from her closet a long dress of soft blue cotton with insets of lace and tiny tucks across the bosom. "This, love, is for you!"

"For me? Oh Mother, is it really for me? Will I have

to give it back?" Monica is speechless with this miracle, that her mother has chosen exactly what she herself would have wanted, had she been allowed to buy a dress. The designer's tag as well as the price tag dangles from the cuff; it is not a cheap dress.

"Go ahead, try it on," Irina says, but she is too late, for Monica has already stripped off her sweater and jeans. The dress fits her perfectly!

"I love it!" she cries, hugging her mother. Oh yes, she does love it! Her father will find her beautiful in it. Still, it's not clear: "Mother, where did you get this?"

"In Victoria. It's brand-new and not a bargain, not on sale either. This time I wanted you to have a perfect dress."

Monica takes it off slowly and carefully, speaks now in a low voice. "You're not becoming a kleptomaniac, are you?" She laughs nervously as she mentions it, although it has crossed her mind that this is possible. Then a new fear: "Oh Mom, you didn't borrow the money from Jim Weed, did you?"

"What's the matter with you, Monica? I earned this dress, paid for it. The Festival Committee argued for two whole hours about what the ushers would wear tomorrow night. It goes without saying that you'll be an usher. I insisted on long feminine dresses and won out. Then I felt as if I'd painted myself into a corner, but I didn't say anything. Just worried. Then . . . oh Monica, life can sometimes be so remarkably hopeful!"

"What happened?"

"Mrs. Heatherington came into the shop, said she was doing her Christmas shopping early. In May, for heaven's sake. Anyway, she bought two crocheted crib covers and ordered a gorgeous mohair shawl and paid for it all in advance! *Voilà*, your dress!"

Monica is touched. "That was so good of her. I'm glad she didn't just give you the money."

"Wait a minute. My work is worth even more than what she paid."

"I know. Oh Mother, you are marvelous, and I thank you."

Secretly she believes that Irina found a flaw in the dress, perhaps a button missing or a slightly ripped seam, for which she argued a healthy reduction in price; it wouldn't be the first time. And yet Irina is gambling heart and soul, and for that very reason it is most likely that she wouldn't skimp in the least, lest it affect her luck.

The doorbell rings and Irina goes down to welcome Jim Weed. Upstairs, alone, Monica puts the dress back on its hanger. The bedroom *is* beautiful, she realizes. A spread of knotted lace rests on a yellow coverlet. Jugs of fragrant lilacs, a caned rocking chair, the gold-framed photograph of that young couple who signed themselves Josef and Irina . . . all this has a sweet country freshness. It also suggests something else.

"A bridal chamber!" she says to herself.

If it works, Irina will be so happy. And if for some reason it doesn't? Monica shivers, then puts the thought out of her mind. She must be positive like her mother. She must have faith. Of course it will work!

With that, she brushes her hair vigorously and decides to call on her old friend Bonnie Robertson.

6

Friends on the Island

Monica borrows her mother's bicycle, and before setting off removes a spider web from the handlebars of the old-fashioned rusty Raleigh and then patiently blows up the tires with a hand pump.

To get to Bonnie's she must ride through Genessee Center, where a weedy patch of grass makes an unconvincing town square surrounded by a small church, two grocery stores that glare at each other, the drugstore where Monica and Bonnie used to dawdle with the boys, and a cluster of six hopeful shops, among them Irina's Knittery with a planter of pink geraniums in front of it.

It has stopped raining, but the whole island drips with moisture—the trees, the skies, the roads, the grass. Monica finally arrives at the Robertsons', a small ranch-type house that would fit properly in any mainland suburb but seems strangely out of place on the Island. Mrs. Robertson answers the door.

"Hello," she says with marked coolness, not even mentioning Monica's name, which she knows well. "Bonnie's in her room."

Before Monica can say good evening, Mrs. Robertson retreats to the kitchen and shuts the door behind her. Ever since Monica won her scholarship, Mrs. Robertson, who used to be so pleasant, has been distant. "Sheer jealousy," Irina explains.

But Bonnie could never be so petty. Why, they had been friends, the best of friends, walking with their arms around each other and whispering secrets. How many times had they practiced strutting and making acceptance speeches for that holiest of days when each believed she would be chosen Festival Queen, Bonnie one year and Monica the next! They had considered themselves closer than sisters then—it was a bond that couldn't be broken.

"Hey, Bonnie! Where are you? It's me," Monica calls up the stairs.

No answer. She is about to call again when Bonnie appears at the top of the stairs. As she stands brushing the silky blonde hair that is her pride over the fluffy pink sweater that clings to her thin body, she seems somehow more grown-up than she did at Christmas vacation.

"Hello, Monica. How are you?" Monica tries not to notice the indifference in her voice. When they last met, Bonnie threw her arms around her.

"Fine. How's everything? I've been wanting to see you. Can't you come down? I thought maybe we could go out for coffee or a Coke or a beer."

Bonnie does not invite Monica up to her room but continues to brush her hair. "I'm afraid I can't. Previous engagement."

Now then, when has Bonnie ever talked like that? Monica senses a new haughtiness in her voice as she continues, "By the way, I'm going to be Festival Queen tomorrow!"

"Terrific! Congratulations. That's wonderful."

In spite of a certain happiness for Bonnie, Monica is aware of a flush of jealousy. Once she considered this the greatest moment possible. So Monica is still an Island girl after all!

"How is everything else, Bonnie?"

"Why would you want to know? Just Island stuff."

"But I care about what's going on. You know that. What's the matter, Bonnie? Can't you come down and talk? Is something wrong?"

"Do I have to spell it out for you? All right, then. First you were too good for the Island, so you went off to the fanciest school you could find. And now you're too good for the Island boys, but you're ready enough to take up with the summer people. I hear that you're really thick with Courtney Phillips, so I just don't know what you'd want with plain old me or any of the real Islanders. Genessee is good enough for us."

"Bonnie, that's stupid! You know better than that. I've never heard such malicious nonsense and I'm amazed that you of all people would believe it—"

She cannot finish her sentence because Bonnie flounces into her room, slamming the door. This is not a fit of temper but a way of saying good-bye.

Monica leaves, gets on her bicycle, and pedals home slowly. Another link with the Island is broken, and she regrets it. Though she has dreamed of leaving the Island, she had not expected she was no longer wanted here. Genessee has the petty cruelties of any small town, she tells herself, and she won't be sorry to leave. At that very moment a deer bounds out of the brush and crosses the road in front of her, and the surprise of it as well as its charming grace pushes this latest disappointment out of her head.

"It's lovely, that deer. Of course I love the Island!"

She pedals faster now along the familiar road, and

then the horn of a car blares in her ear and sends her bolting to the edge of the road. The car stops and she is flooded with relief to see that it is the Rover and that Courtney is driving it.

"Monica! I've been looking all over for you. Get in. I've got to get some beer and pretzels for the family . . . can you imagine, forgetting beer! After that I'm free."

He gets out and helps her put the bicycle in the back of the car. Monica slips in beside him. At the Center he goes into a grocery store and comes out with both arms laden—at least five dollars' worth of pretzels and heaven alone knows how much for the beer, and he thinks nothing of it. It's the way the girls at school spend money, and Monica hates herself for noticing it.

He chatters all the way to the West Shore, where, he promises, he will drop off the beer and come right back to the car.

"Why didn't we ever get together in Vancouver? I called you at least six times," he asks when he returns.

"I couldn't go that time just before exams. I guess not all your calls came through. I tried to find you once. Impossible!"

"We'll have to have a bash before the year is over," he says. "Doesn't it get dull if you stay in that place all the time?"

"Right! Sometimes I think I'm in a convent. Getting permission to go out is a hassle. Still, it's possible."

She smiles winsomely, anticipating an evening in the city with Court. She remembers but does not tell him of the one time when she left the campus without permission.

It was during March. The school was planning its annual Parents' Night, when the girls would appear in long dresses, dine at the school with their parents, and afterward attend a program to be climaxed by the giving of awards. Monica would be getting one in math, and so she had written to her father a month before to invite him. Each day she awaited an answer to her letter or a telephone call. Nothing.

Calling home from campus involved too many questions from the headmistress, so one evening she put on jeans and a raincoat, anonymous enough attire, and escaped through a break in the gate at the back of a field. She ran for a mile or so to be safely away from the school, caught a bus, and rode to the city center. How wonderfully alive and brilliant it seemed! She was a city person after all, but the important thing was to call her father. She wanted so much for him to say yes, of course he would come, that she could actually imagine his voice and the very words he would use.

She slipped into the Hotel Vancouver and called him at home. A girl—or was it a young woman?—with a cool distant voice, a faintly English accent, said matter-of-factly that the professor wasn't there, would she like him to return the call? Disappointed that he was not there, Monica practically whispered the question: "Do you know if he is planning to come to Vancouver next week?"

"No, I don't believe so. At least, I know nothing about it. Who is this?"

Monica put the receiver back. Then she was angry, furious; he hadn't even bothered to answer the invitation.

And he wasn't even there when she had taken

such a risk to try to reach him! Unreasonable as this last might have been, she no longer delighted in the city. She caught the bus back to the school and reached her room safely.

It wasn't until the night of the banquet that it occurred to her that she should have asked Irina; she hadn't even thought of it.

She is still feeling guilty about this, one of the many things she should have done but didn't, when Courtney returns to the car. "Where to, Monica?"

"Let's go to my house, Courtney," she says. "Don't you want to say hello to my mother? She'd love to see you."

"Can't resist that," he says, and the rain comes down again in wet splattering drops as they drive to Bittersweet Place.

———7

A Little Night Party

"Come in, darlings! Oh my, you're wet. That rain, it would have to rain! Courtney, so good to see you!"

Irina sweeps across the room to greet them, holding out both hands to Courtney, gracious and charming. "Can she be flirting with him?" Monica wonders.

"Mother, I didn't know you were going to have a party."

"Neither did I," she says lightheartedly. "Kathryn came over with a big potful of mulled wine and of course Jim was here, and then Tom and Dennis came, and so it goes. You all know Monica, of course, and do you all know Courtney Phillips? Here he is!" she says, turning to the guests, who smile up at the couple.

"Have you ever seen two more handsome kids!" someone says. Immediately Monica is embarrassed, feels everyone looking at them, and blushes at a complimentary murmur of voices, but Courtney takes the flattery easily. His manners are perfect, so very perfect —he must have been born with them, Monica thinks.

The fire flickers in the fireplace, sending out woodsy odors and reflecting kindly Irina and her friends, who sit around on cushions as they drink the cinnamon wine. Irina finds a place for Monica and Courtney, and then sits in the armchair, for she must finish this baby sweater and tie the knots on that afghan and lace some booties, for these items are to be sold the next day. Her fingers work with incredible speed and cleverness, yet she sits calmly and regally, like a queen. Imagine daring to wear a white woolen skirt while making a fire! No, Monica thinks, not a queen but the mistress of a salon, for she says little but somehow manages to hold these individuals together. It has always been like this with Irina. She is an Island countess . . . that's it exactly, Monica thinks.

". . . And tomorrow you must come and see Wunderkind," Dennis is saying. "I swear, you will never see such a spectacular goat. She's marked like an oriental rug, so help me. Exotic creature!"

Dennis and Tom, who have traveled all over the world and have done everything from theater to teaching in a boys' school to collecting antiques, have settled here in Genessee to run a goat farm. Strange sophistications!

Fireplace talk. Anecdotes, small confessions, some Island gossip, of course, speculations, and enthusiasm for the little theater.

". . . an experimental play this summer. What about it, Monica? Courtney? You must try out."

"But Irina must take the lead. There's a part for her, and nobody else can do it. Monica, you must convince your mother . . ."

Irina laughs but her eyes, which catch Monica's, warn her not to tell that they might not be here this summer after all.

Two of Louka's kittens wobble across the floor. Kathryn refills everyone's glasses while Jim Weed puts another log on the fire. It is getting late, Courtney whispers to Monica. He should go, but oh this is a marvelous party! Tom and Dennis begin to sing, and they sing well, an Irish ballad. Irina, sharper than ever, joins them in the chorus as she folds garments and ties knots on a shawl. Courtney is enchanted and cannot keep his eyes away from her.

One song leads to another and the log burns brilliantly in the fireplace. They have begun their fifth song —it will be an endless night—when Gabrielle bursts in, rain dripping from her slicker, and drops the airline bag on the floor. She resembles an illustration from a children's book.

"There she is!"

"Got caught in the rain, did you?"

"Come sit by me, Gaby, honey. I'll keep you warm."

"Darling, I thought you were going to be with Rosemary tonight."

"I want to be with Monica," Gabrielle insists, "and

with you. I just *knew* you'd have a party. And you didn't even ask me."

"Aww, poor Gaby!"

"Poor Gaby" snuggles beside Courtney, another song is sung; but Kathryn gets up after that and soon everyone is bundling into parkas, raincapes, and jackets. They hug the girls and kiss Irina, who has never been more loving.

"Mrs. Kroll, you are magnificent!" Courtney cries, his eyes sparkling.

"Hear, hear!" Tom cries, while Irina pulls Courtney toward her and kisses him on both cheeks. "You are a darling!" she says. "You must come again soon!"

As everyone leaves, Irina stands with her daughters in the doorway. We must look like a tableau, Monica supposes, "Mother with Daughters." When the last car has left, Irina cries:

"Let's go to bed. Tomorrow is already here!"

"So soon?" Monica can hardly believe it, but Gabrielle is half asleep. Irina turns out the lights and they all go upstairs.

8

Good Night

Monica falls asleep quickly, but an hour later she is awake again. Not three feet away Gabrielle sleeps among her dolls and teddy bears; safe in the capsule of a dream, she breathes softly and rhythmically, innocent as a Florentine angel.

The fitful rain has stopped again, but the wind has blown open the casement windows and the white bedroom curtains toss themselves out wantonly on the night air. The night is as wild and romantic as a Liszt concerto. The maple sighs, the willow bends in the wind, and the moon races furiously across the sky, now hiding, now striking out in full view before disappearing again.

She wishes she could pray that it will all turn out as they wish, but she has never learned to pray and cannot quite begin now. As she hovers between wakefulness and sleep, an image takes the place of prayer. Her father stands with his arm around her mother while she and Gabrielle lean against the railing of a ship that gleams white in the blue water. Someone has said something amusing and Tom and Dennis are singing a farewell song as *The Genessee Queen* carries them away. All their friends, everyone they have known on Genessee Island, even Bonnie and her mother, stand on shore and wave good-bye, for they are leaving and will never come back.

Content with that, Monica curls up and sleeps soundly until the next morning.

PART THREE

The Genessee Festival

_____1

Morning

The sun chooses to sulk behind overladen clouds, but as far as Monica is concerned, it might as well be blazing. This is the day that her father comes! Gabrielle sighs in her sleep: an admission of hidden troubles? Let her sleep, then, but for Monica sleep is impossible. She slips into a faded quilted robe and tiptoes quietly across the cold linoleum floor and down the stairs, being careful to avoid the step that would shriek like a pistol shot in the early morning silence.

"Mother?" she calls softly, but there is no answer. Yet she must be up, for the coffee is perking deliciously in the battered percolator. Monica begins to collect the half-emptied glasses and plates from last night's party on a tray, then catches sight of Irina in the garden. Monica puts down the tray and stands idly at the window. Louka jumps on her shoulder and together they watch Irina, who stands in the wet grass and then reaches forward to snip a branch of yellow forsythia.

Now the question that once bothered Monica is answered; without doubt Irina is truly beautiful. She stands there in a typically "Irinaish" costume—a lavender robe with a trimming of lace; rubber boots; and, on her head, a green felt hat with slouching brim, her "great Garbo" hat. She has already gathered an armful of white, lavender, and purple lilacs, stalks of yellow forsythia, and sprays of white bridal veil, which are perfect in themselves, yet she contemplates a single spike of deep blue delphinium. The black hair that hangs down her back is a vertical accent to the scene, which is as rich as an Impressionist painting. How Manet or Renoir would have loved Irina!

Suddenly aware that she is being watched, Irina turns to the window, waves enthusiastically, and, leaving the delphinium after all, hurries to the porch.

"Hello, my darling, hello! This is the day!" she calls out. How gay and hopeful we are this morning, she indicates with every gesture of the long thin body as she plunges the flowers deep into a pail of lukewarm water.

"That will ease the shock. Poor things, being cut off from their life source like that!" she explains to Monica. She pulls off her boots and walks over to give her daughter a double good-morning kiss, one on each cheek.

Later Irina will turn the house into a flower shop of bouquets from these blooms, using everything from beer bottles to a choice pottery vase of Kathryn's, and each arrangement will be deftly made and as perfect as a Dutch still life. Flowers for the returning hero!

"This is *the* day. Our day, love! Have you said a prayer? Even if you don't pray, this day deserves a prayer."

"Want me to light a candle?"

"Anything is all right, if only it works. And of course it will work! Is the coffee ready? There's toast and some of the plum jam we made last summer. Oh Monica, I'm so glad, so happy! I know it's going to be the beginning of something new and wonderful for all of us."

She touches Monica's cheek with a long slender hand. "Some daughter!"

"Some mother!" Monica answers. It is true. Irina is unique among mothers. As they sip the coffee, which is nearly too hot and too strong, if such is possible, Monica remembers something important.

"You never told me, Mother, what ferry Daddy will take to get here. Are we all going to meet him at the dock?"

"The two o'clock ferry, but I'm afraid we won't be meeting him there. You can guess who made all the arrangements. The limousine will be there to pick up the trio. The Pouter Pigeon saw to that."

"That's not very nice of her. Shouldn't we be there waiting for him?"

"With the Genessee Brass Band to welcome the trio? Really, Monica. Mrs. H. made it very clear that this is a professional engagement and not a family affair." Irina cannot help but imitate the prestigious Mrs. H. as she talks about her. "Anyway, I have a million things to do at the Festival."

"I'll help you, Mom," Monica promises. But she vows that she will meet her father at the dock, no matter what Mrs. Heatherington decrees. After all, Monica has been waiting for a long time for the ecstatic moment when he will walk down the gangplank from the ferry to Genessee.

2

The Long Drizzly
Morning of the Festival

Booths have been set up along one end of the school yard, not far from Bittersweet Place, and the Festival is already under way when Irina and Monica arrive, arms loaded down with Irina's harvest of crocheted articles. On the far side of the pasture, pits have been dug and fires begun for the lambs that will be barbecued all during the day. The mooing of cows and the baaing of sheep that have been herded into stalls for the livestock exhibition compete with the voices of the men who are testing the speaker system from the platform that has been erected in the center of the pasture.

Monica remembers the other Festivals—the fragrance of the fires, the chorus of animals, and the excitement of people arriving. Even the chilly moistness of the air is familiar and good. She almost regrets that this will be her last Festival here.

"I'm afraid we'll have to put everything inside the booth. I'd hoped that today of all days it wouldn't rain. I wanted to hang the ponchos out here," Irina complains.

"They'll look brilliant anywhere. Nobody will be able to resist them," Monica assures her as they set about pinning up the shawls, skirts, and sweaters. More accurately, nobody will be able to miss them, Monica thinks; the booth wears the aspect of a blazing exhibition in a modern museum. But these items, which would be daring and innovative elsewhere, will appear bizarre to most of the Islanders and Monica fears they will not sell. Fortunately, Irina has knitted and crocheted baby booties, baby sweaters, crib covers, and other such items in conventional styles and colors, and these may do well for her. The booth appears to show the work of two separate people—a bold, daring artist and a timid housewife.

In a long red woolen skirt, embroidered shirt, and luxurious mohair stole, Irina herself stands out from the crowd that is beginning to gather. The Festival has scarcely begun, but already several visitors have come up to ask Irina if they may take a picture of her. She poses theatrically and gracefully. A bevy of Brownies run up to beg Irina to help them solve some last-minute problem as a harassed-looking woman rushes up to ask Irina what can be done about some flags. Do they dare put them up with the threat of rain in the skies?

"Would you take the booth, dear, for just a little while?" Irina begs prettily as she rushes off to help these people and see about other last-minute arrangements. How surprising that so many people actually depend on the scatterbrained Irina! Monica is continually amazed and comforted by this.

And what will her father think of the Island and of the Festival? Monica tries to see it through his eyes. Nearby an enormous brown steer growls ominously as he lies in the large wooden stall that has been erected for his benefit. Later that day he will be raffled off and most likely he will be led to the butcher's before nightfall. Will her father find this as savage and revolting as she does? This is the dark side of these smiling hardy

Islanders, the side that makes her forever a stranger to them.

Two boys she once knew at school almost walk on by the booth, then recognize her and stop to talk.

"Hey, Monica, it's you! Boy, I thought you'd left for good."

"Not for good, Tommy. Hi, Ken!"

"She remembers us, Tommy! Hey, you still going to that school? How do you like it?"

"It's okay. How is it here? Anything new?"

"Naw. Nothin' ever changes here. I might get a motorcycle."

They chew gum, gawk at Irina's wilder sweaters, and then, as there doesn't seem to be anything more to talk about, they say "See ya" to Monica and shuffle off.

"Miss, Miss, I'd like to see that sweater. No, not that one, the pink one."

Two women in pink polyester pantsuits are standing in front of her. Monica unfolds the sweater carefully, as though it were a masterpiece, whispers the price modestly when they ask what it is, and suffers their comments.

"High enough. I could make it for lots less. But I guess it's pin money for some. Might as well take it," she says grudgingly as she takes a bill from her purse. Monica wants to cry that this is their living, that it will buy their bread and butter that summer, but restrains herself, thanks the woman with an insincere smile, and points out that Irina's work is unique—if she will just notice the detail of the joining here and the edging there.

"You could do it yourself cheaper, Alma," the companion mutters as they walk away.

Everyone comes to see Irina's handiwork, but people

buy little except the booties and simpler scarves. Then Crazy Hattie, one of the Island solitaries, who talks to herself and mumbles obscene curses as she walks about the Island, stands in front of the display, and her loose lower lip forms something that resembles a smile as she praises one of Irina's wilder skirts with its mad splotches of red, violet, and green. "Tell yer mother she's okay. She's good. You tell her I said so."

"I will," Monica promises, adding to herself, "if I ever see her again."

But within a few minutes Irina floats over to the booth. "My darling, let me free you now so you can see all your friends—and be sure to visit Dennis's goat, and don't forget to change your clothes this afternoon. See you later!"

As Monica walks over the uneven terrain toward the livestock, she is constantly greeted by people. Three of her former teachers here, the old man with a shock of white hair who runs the fish market, and the two retired actresses with their silver slippers and half-inch false eyelashes stop to say hello. Three of the summer people from the West Shore stop to exclaim over her. These are the women for whom she has cleaned house and baby-sat, and now they beg her to work for them again this summer; one of them asks if it is her father who will be performing that evening, and they say isn't it wonderful for the Island to have such distinguished musicians, and is her mother selling those marvelous crocheted things this year. Visitors swarm around the pasture. It will take her forever to get to Dennis's goats, but she is almost there when a small Japanese woman taps her on the shoulder.

"Mrs. Tanaka! How good to see you!" She hugs this

small woman whose glasses keep sliding down her tiny nose; and the three young children, brown with crow-black hair, jump up and down around Monica until she has to bend down and greet each one.

"When you come see us, Monica? Garden good this year. You home for good?"

"No, only a short vacation."

"But you must come and see us," Mr. Tanaka insists. "We will want to hear all about school."

Mrs. Tanaka says something in Japanese to him.

"Yes, we are pleased your father will be playing a concert. It's a great honor."

"Don't forget, come see us," Mrs. Tanaka repeats.

"I promise, I'll come," Monica cries, wishing she could take her father there, for the Tanaka place is a jewel—a low brown farmhouse set in a natural garden beside three acres of carefully grown flowers and vegetables, which are sold in Vancouver and Victoria at premium rates. It is the garden around the house that she loves the most, for it appears natural in its green mossiness—a meditative place where she has often sat sipping tea with the Tanakas, nibbling tiny salty cookies, and reading to the children. A peaceful place.

Would her father see it as she does, as something to be desired?

"My dear, aren't you going to watch your sister perform in the ballet? She'll be broken-hearted if you're not there." Aunt Kathryn, in a blue raincoat and weathered hat, has slipped her arm around Monica.

"She hardly mentioned it. But I've *got* to take a look at Dennis's goats. Can we hurry there first?"

"Let's rush, then. I couldn't bear to miss Gabrielle as a butterfly."

Dennis, in a brightly embroidered jacket, greets them and shows off his goats, particularly his prize kid.

"Ooooh, she's a darling. Can I hold her, Dennis, please?" Monica cries. "She really *does* look like an oriental rug. I've never seen such markings. And I like the others too. Oh Dennis, they're all so beautiful!"

"You'll have to become a goat farmer, then." Dennis grins. "You can come and help me milk any time."

Her father would not like that, she decides, but it doesn't matter. He would think the goats smelled, though they don't. She is seeing everything through his eyes. He would admire this handsome ageless woman, this Kathryn who now makes apologies to Dennis for leaving so quickly, but they mustn't miss the ballet.

"One minute, Monica," Kathryn says as they walk back toward the grandstand. Monica catches a sober note in her voice, stops to listen.

"I know you're excited about your father's coming. You haven't seen him for a long time. But darling, don't expect too much now. Remember, he's only human."

"Well, of course."

"What I mean is that when you're away from some-one for a long time it's easy to forget that changes occur or that perhaps the person is not quite so perfect as you may have imagined. Do you understand?"

"Kathryn, I'm not worried. Everything is going to be fine. I've never been so sure about anything. It's going to work out for him, for my mother, for Gabrielle and me. It even makes me sad to think that this may be my last Festival Day."

"Uh-huh." Kathryn smiles noncommittally and then,

as a tinny piano and a raw country violin strike up a waltz, cries, "Here they are!"

Five little girls, Gabrielle among them, skip onto the platform in leotards with tie-dyed sheets attached to their wrists to represent butterfly wings. All except Gabrielle are husky butterflies and unintentionally bump into one another from time to time with audible smacks. They wobble as they each balance on one foot and raise their arms above their heads. One poor butterfly has lost a wing; it drags disconsolately behind her. But Gabrielle is remarkable! Why, she really is a dancer, Monica realizes for the first time. She dances lightly and easily with a stage presence, a mysterious magnetism, that makes her slightest movement inexpressibly beautiful.

"She's terrific, isn't she? I never realized it before," Monica says, and something else occurs to her. "Kathryn, we can't let her go to waste here on the Island."

Kathryn nods wisely. "Exactly," she says.

"Hey, yer mother wants ya," a small boy tells Monica.

"Thanks. Have to go now, Kathryn," Monica explains. She rushes back to the booth, where her mother is adjusting a line of makeup around her large green eyes and powdering her long thin nose. A quick curve of lipstick over her mouth, and then she sees Monica.

"If you don't mind taking over the booth, I'm supposed to be singing now."

"You're singing in public, Mother? Are you serious?"

Irina draws herself up. "And why not? I've been invited," she states, her voice growing peppery. She disappears as two stout, firmly trussed visitors in flowered dresses come to the booth to examine the baby blankets.

Soon Irina is on the platform, smiling broadly, striking a few chords on the guitar, and singing Black, black, black is the color of my true love's hair. The sound system falters, then exaggerates Irina's sharp notes, and Monica prays that her mother will not sing when her father is here; it will ruin everything.

Monica is about to show the ladies one of her mother's quieter shawls when a pair of hands covers her eyes, glasses and all. The low laugh betrays Courtney, and Monica wheels around to see him dressed for the Festival in a fringed pioneer jacket and leather hat, genuinely antique.

"Courtney! You look marvelous!"

She will introduce him to her father. Oh yes, this is a handsome young man who now hovers over her and begs her to come to lunch with him. Irina sings another song that is too highly pitched, and the sound system betrays her, translating the high note a full tone sharp. She gestures as though this were high opera. Then the whistle of a passing ship blows shrilly, competing with poor Irina. The ladies cover their ears with their hands.

"This is giving me a headache. Let's go, Margaret!"

And so another sale is lost. It begins to rain. Again Courtney begs her to stand in line with him so they can have that marvelous lamb. He sniffs appreciatively. But she cannot think of food; in less than two hours her father will come! She smiles regretfully at Courtney.

"Someone's got to mind the store. Later, all right?"

"I'll see you later, then. Don't forget, now!"

She watches him stride away. Halfway across the field he turns and waves to her. He *is* quite perfect, she thinks. Her father will be pleased.

3

Gabrielle's Hat

Gabrielle runs up to the booth with Valerie and Rosemary. She has abandoned her butterfly costume but the makeup still paints her face; it is incongruous with the light cotton shorts she wears and the bulky gray sweater that makes her wiry body appear huge, like the body of an insect with long thin arms and legs. All three girls are eating pink fluffy cotton candy. Gross, so gross, Monica thinks, and yet she was doing this herself only two years ago.

"My hat, I gotta have my hat!" Gabrielle complains. "The contest's pretty soon."

"You mean you haven't done anything about it since last night?"

Gabrielle shakes her head. "Mama's busy and wants you to do it."

"But I've got to stay here. Where *is* Mother, anyway?"

Gabrielle shrugs her shoulders and skips off, and the other girls follow. Five minutes later she skips back, pulling along Jim Weed.

"I guess you're sorely needed. I'll take over, if you like," he says.

"Jim, you are so nice." She has almost said "too nice," which is more like it, but has decided "so nice" will have to do. It's all for love of Irina, Monica knows, that Jim is forever helping her out, but she cannot stop to think of the fairness and unfairness of love now.

"Thanks so much!" she cries, and promises to be back soon. Then she runs with her sister. One of Gabrielle's other friends is already in the house playing the same piano pieces that Gabrielle played the night before, with just as many errors and hesitations.

"Come *on*, Monica. Hurry up!"

The basket that is the base for the hat has disappeared and nobody can find a needle, thread, a thimble, scissors. The objects that will decorate the hat are as yet unassembled. Yet they have had weeks to prepare the hat! This is another side of Irina, that nothing is where it ought to be and that what should be done has been forgotten. Jim Weed finds this charming; Monica doesn't.

At that very moment Valerie rings the bell and enters wearing her contest hat, an elegant wide-brimmed straw on which rests a garden of flowers, both real and artificial; a Japanese silk butterfly sways on a wire extending from a luxurious cabbage rose. This child with the soft pale curls and innocent china-blue eyes reminds Monica of those girls at Chatham who are so tenderly nurtured that they cannot imagine what it would be like to be a Monica or a Gabrielle. Lucky girls to be so carefully tended, to be as lovely and fragile as hothouse blooms!

"Monica, stop staring at Valerie and *make my hat*."

"Okay, pumpkin. Let's look for the stuff: basket, needle, thread. Quick!"

The thread turns up on the pantry shelf, the pin cushion among her mother's cosmetics in the bathroom, and the basket has been tossed into a corner on the porch to become a bed for Louka's sleeping kittens.

"We'll make you a gorgeous hat. Wait and see!" Monica promises as she collects a long green ribbon, parsley from the garden, and from the refrigerator a bunch of radishes and some sprigs of broccoli. It will be a vegetable garden to match Valerie's flowers, but Gabrielle objects.

"No, I want a *garbage* hat like Mama said. I want the prize."

"Don't be so greedy. Wouldn't you rather be beautiful?"

Gabrielle makes a nasty noise. Against her better judgment, Monica sews on peels from a quartered orange and the tin lid from a can of tomato soup. She sews quickly and soon Gabrielle is posing before the mirror, pulling the hat first this way and then that.

"There, I'm going to win the prize," she says haughtily in a voice that is an unmistakable imitation of Mrs. Heatherington's. Again Monica has an intuition about her sister: she will become an actress, a dancer, someone who must be admired.

"Come on, I'm starving. I want something to *eat*," the pristine Valerie cries.

The girls argue over whether they should get hot dogs or barbecued lamb. Gabrielle passes the dollar her mother has given her for lunch in front of Monica's eyes, a little girl boasting "See what I've got!" Then she surprises Monica with a warm embrace, the thin arms entwined around her sister's neck, and an impulsive kiss on the cheek.

"Thanks for the hat, Monica. You're terrific. It's just what I wanted. And *don't forget to come and watch!*" she cries. Finally she runs off with her friends. The house echoes with their chatter and then falls silent.

4

To the Harbor

The time has flown and if she does not hurry, she will miss the arrival of the ferry. Of all the hard luck! There isn't even time to change into the long skirt and shirt she had laid out for the occasion; indeed, hardly enough time to throw on her white wool poncho, one of Irina's finest efforts, and pass a brush through her hair. She catches a glimpse of herself in the mirror as she rushes to the garage and pulls out the bicycle. Immediately she decides to take the back road that leads to the harbor, for it is actually shorter and apt to be less crowded than the main road, but the hills are steep and curved. The important matter is to get there in time.

The woods along this twisting back road are inhospitable, with ugly NO TRESPASSING signs on the tall thin trunks. In winter this area is a black forest of vertical charcoal tree trunks with a tangle of branches above. Even now, in May, the leaves are reluctant to unfurl; they are slower than those of the other trees on the Island. A black crow follows Monica, flying above her and cawing down at her.

Can this be an omen of some impending disaster?

"In a novel it would be," she thinks, "but what of it? This isn't exactly a story. It's real. Only good things will happen." She is reassuring herself of this just as a car zooms past, sending her bicycle off the road, where she falls in a patch of wet leaf mold. She cries out; she is presently aware of her arm hurting and of her heart thumping loudly long after the car has disappeared.

But she is still alive! Her arm may be sore, but surely is not broken. Now she is grateful to be whole, for if she were to miss seeing her father now, she could not bear it.

Her white poncho is badly smeared with mud and fragments of leaves. Her face must be dirty as well. Damn! she cries. What will her father think? She brushes herself off as well as she can, pushes her bicycle to the top of the hill, and once again finds new symbols, hopeful signs. Venerable cedars replace the snarl and tangle of the black forest she has just passed, and, more wonderful still, the sun has come out—a timid sun, a low-watt bulb in the sky. From her perch on the hill Monica watches *The Genessee Queen* turn the bend and sail toward shore.

She mounts the bicycle and lets it speed down the hill. The wind rushes through her hair and the poncho flies out behind her. The bicycle performs proudly and neither slows down nor breaks down, but takes her right to the dock, where she gets off and mingles with a crowd of young people in drab skirts and the ubiquitous jeans. Now Monica wonders if her father will recognize her, or if she will appear to him only as one of the crowd.

A flurry of excitement runs through the crowd as Mrs. Heatherington's long black limousine, purring royally, moves into an open space at the harbor. Simon, the chauffeur, gets out and waits for the musicians, arms folded. He wears his chauffeur's hat now; in his straw hat he is Mrs. Heatherington's gardener, and on other occasions, when he is hatless, he becomes her butler.

The ferry settles in her berth, creaks between the piles; the chains are taken away, the ramp dropped, and then the foot passengers walk out. With what hilarity the new set of vacationers meet the people who surround Monica; they hug one another and slowly leave. Other passengers come off the ferry now. But where is her father? Her hand flies to her throat in alarm.

And then she sees him! Her heart beats like the wings of an excited bird and the blood rushes to her head, then falls away so rapidly she is afraid she may faint, although of course she knows she will do nothing of the sort. Her father is not half so tall as she remembers him, nor so slim—nor as young. Still, she is quick to defend him: he is not really fat, simply a little rounder than before, an aging Valentino. His hair is too gray at the sideburns and the temples and too black elsewhere—a terrible dye job. Instantly she thinks that Irina would do it much more subtly; perhaps he needs her after all. His clothes are splendid, though, sophisticated and expensive, a tailored suede jacket and lightly checked pants. He still has a certain flair.

No, he has not changed much. He walks the same, very erect, with his violin case tucked under his arm. He chats casually with the tall young man who strides along beside him; this must be the cellist, of course, for he carries the large case lightly; he looks around the Island pleasantly. Monica supposes that the small pale girl who walks on the other side of her father is the pianist, and she is surprised that her father has chosen someone who is so slight and colorless.

His eyes pass over her but he does not seem to see

her. Should she rush forward and cry, "Daddy, here I am! It's me, Monica!"? Two years ago she might have done just that, her voice fluttering with emotion, but now she knows it is too dramatic, too operatic, altogether too unbecoming. It would only embarrass her poor father, so she stands there and waits.

His eyes flicker over her again and she is sure that he actually sees her, but it's clear that he does not recognize her. At that moment Simon approaches the musicians and asks respectfully if this is the trio—a safe assumption, since the two men carry instrument cases and the girl carries music. Simon helps them with their luggage and instruments and holds the door of the limousine for them.

Monica stands rigidly still, staring at him; then her view is blocked by the passing of two bicyclists and five matronly women in the white outfits of the Lawn Bowling Association. Just before the car pulls out, Josef, aware that he is being watched, waves and nods his head in her direction as though she were an admirer who recognized a celebrity, nothing more.

As the limousine drives away she consoles herself. It's just as well he didn't recognize her, for her poncho is stained, her face is probably dirty still, and she might have cried with emotion had he come to her, and then everyone would have been embarrassed—more embarrassed than touched, she believes. In any event, Mrs. Heatherington has promised to bring the celebrities to the Festival for the crowning of the Festival Queen at four o'clock, and now she will have to rush home to get herself ready for the occasion. A hot shower, fresh clothes, a touch of Irina's perfume, and her father will say, "Can this be Monica?" Yes, it's just as well he didn't know her. She jumps on her bicycle and pedals toward Bittersweet Place.

_____5

Hello, Dad, Remember Me?

At home she takes a long steaming shower to purify herself before meeting her father, then changes to clean underwear, a long patched jean skirt, a red bandana shirt, boots (from the Goodwill, but serviceable and chic, a lucky find), and a short blue corduroy cape (also from the Goodwill) to replace the white poncho. As she brushes her hair, the door slams downstairs, and a burst of little-girl laughter and someone banging "Chopsticks" on the piano breaks the silence. Gabrielle rushes upstairs and sits down heavily on her bed. She pouts unprettily.

"Guess who won first prize in that dumb hat contest."

"Valerie?" Monica asks.

"No, she didn't get anything. Mary Sykes got first, and guess what she wore? A _real_ garbage can, with banana peels, egg shells, and a rotten stalk of celery, just like Mama said."

"Sounds ugly to me. You thought so too last night. Did you want to be ugly?"

"I wanted to win the prize. First prize."

"Who got second?"

"I did, but I really wanted first."

Monica sits down beside her, puts an arm around her. "And you're complaining? Look, sweetie, it was a dumb contest. You should get a prize for dancing. You were sensational this morning. Do you ever think about becoming a dancer?"

She shrugs her shoulders. "I'd rather have a horse."

What is one to do with her? But then, Monica realizes, Gabrielle has never seen professional dancing. Well, then, they will both go back to California and Gabrielle will see a genuine ballet, go to a good ballet school, and not waste herself. Like Irina did, Monica adds to herself, though Irina has long since stopped caring.

Rosemary shouts up the stairwell. "C'mon, Gaby, it's time to go. They're gonna crown the Festival Queen."

"Wait a minute, you can't go like that," Monica says to Gabrielle. "Daddy's coming. Remember? Don't you want to change your clothes?"

She holds out a skirt and one of Irina's handsome blue sweaters, but Gabrielle turns up her nose.

"I like what I'm wearing now," she insists. Those awful summer shorts, that thrift-shop shirt the letters of which—DANGER, KEEP OUT—have not faded enough.

"Gaby, don't you want your father to be proud of you?"

"He'll be proud enough, and anyway, I don't think he cares."

Monica is taken aback by this, her first shocked reaction being that Gabrielle may be right, but she says, "Of course he cares." Gabrielle sighs in exasperation and changes to a shirt that says HORSES ARE BEAUTIFUL, replaces the basket-hat on her head. At this point it does resemble a garbage receptacle, but it's clear she intends to wear it.

"Let's go," Monica says. "Does Irina never take care of Gabrielle?" she wonders. She gives Gabrielle a quick smile and a hug; then the two of them run toward the Festival grounds.

Aunt Kathryn is manning the booth. "It's all right," she tells Monica, "I don't mind. Irina's gone off to judge a dog show, but she'll be back."

"Dogs? What does she know about dogs?"

"Oh well, you know Irina. She's popular. She can act as if she knows all about dogs!" Kathryn comments with a wry grin.

Courtney sees Monica and dashes over. "Where have you been? Good lord, I've been waiting for you."

He has never appeared so possessive before. "I'm sorry," she apologizes.

"Tell me, Monica, where *were* you?" he insists.

"I went down to the dock to see my father land."

"Oh, so you got to see your father? How did it go?"

"I just saw him land. There wasn't any time really," she says as casually as she can manage, not really wanting to discuss this with Courtney, and he does not persist in questioning her.

"Look, isn't that Mrs. Heatherington's limo?" she cries as the black car rolls down the country road toward the gate. It is then that Monica hears a thin nasal voice call her. "Oh Monica, Monica!"

She claps her hands over her ears and hopes she has only imagined that she has heard Sheila, but there she is in her school uniform, a canvas suitcase at her side, and her face shining with a big grin. "I told you I'd come, Monica, and here I am! I took the ferry all by myself.

My mother was nearly hysterical and my father was awfully cross, but I just wouldn't go back home. So here I am! Is this Courtney?"

Monica wills herself to introduce them, but she is ready to tear this exasperating girl to shreds. All this time she has been urging Sheila to act as an individual and of course it is just like her to choose this one moment to do so—the very worst time. She cannot have Sheila hanging around her now when she is about to meet her father.

"Pardon me, but could I talk with Sheila alone for just a minute? You won't mind, will you, Courtney?"

If anything, Courtney appears relieved. The usually silent Sheila has been chattering constantly. "Of course. I'll see you later." His impeccable poise and friendly smile stay Monica's frustration; she will not shake her roommate until her teeth rattle after all.

"Sheila," she begins in a low controlled voice that is close to shaking, "it's great that you got away, but I told you, my *father* is coming. In fact he's coming now, in that limousine. We haven't seen him for years, and there isn't any room at our house. No room, do you understand?"

"I thought you wanted me to come," she pouts.

"I did, Sheila. I mean I do. I want to show you the Island and go walking with you and all that, but not now. Can't you understand? What am I going to do with you?"

Sheila sniffles and looks down at her shoes, playing the role of the child victim, and Monica is beside herself with nervousness and exasperation. "I can just go home again," Sheila says.

"No, no, of course not. Don't do that!" Monica cries, and then, feeling a friendly arm around her shoulders, she turns to see that Aunt Kathryn has come. Blessed, blessed Aunt Kathryn! She will understand.

"Aunt Kathryn, this is my roommate, Sheila. Can she call you Aunt Kathryn too?"

"I'd be delighted. Hello, Sheila. Welcome to the Island! I think your father is coming now, Monica, and I offered to take over the booth so you and your mother could be free. Sheila, think you could come and help me out?"

"Well . . ." Sheila is about to object, but Monica smiles encouragingly, takes her arm, and guides her behind the counter. Then, to keep her from being hurt, she hugs her and promises they will get together later, after her father leaves. Aunt Kathryn assures Monica that she is glad of the opportunity to meet Sheila, and now Monica must leave, because Courtney does seem to be waiting for her, and the black limousine is rolling across the field toward the grandstand.

"See you later," Monica promises, and rushes off to catch a glimpse of her father.

First the chauffeur must help Mrs. Heatherington out of the car as carefully as if she were a stick of dynamite that could go off at any second, and then the trio emerges. How nattily her father is dressed—a pale yellow vest under the suede jacket, and the French beret that becomes him so well! She is proud of him, yes, so very proud! The little pianist stands beside him, dull and colorless, though her gray pantsuit is well tailored. The tall young cellist is truly gawky and yet charming, glancing about in surprise, as though he had suddenly found himself in the center of a stage set.

Monica begins to walk over to her father, but she cannot meet him yet, for Mrs. Heatherington, very much the dowager today in a brown-flowered chiffon

dress and a high, firmly planted hat the ribbons of
which shake in the wind, leads the band and urges
everyone to sing the Island song, "O Genessee, My
Genessee!" Monica sings obediently while her eyes
never leave her father, whose eyes comb the crowd. He
is looking for us, Monica believes—but not very hard,
for he is soon whispering with the young pianist.

"Welcome, welcome all to the Genessee Island Festival!" Mrs. Heatherington bellows through the tem-
peramental sound system; she speaks slowly, pronounc-
ing each syllable as though her audience were either
deaf or not very bright, and as she talks a cow moos
from her stall and the sheep begin to bleat.

Monica cannot very well interrupt the grand lady,
whose sharp eyes would certainly chide Monica should
she dash over to her father now. With horror she hears
the announcement that the children of the first and second grades will sing a song of welcome under the
guidance of Irina Kroll. So her mother has arranged for
her former husband to see her as a performer, someone
to be applauded. And now the gypsy mother in her red
skirt and embroidered shirt leads twenty small children
onto the platform. Oh how beautiful she can be, and
how absolutely victorious she is as her eyes sweep the
crowd and she smiles—but please, God, don't let her
sing! Monica holds her breath, but some guardian of
common sense permits Irina only to strike the appropriate chords on her guitar and mouth the words, in
case the children forget; she does not sing. The children's voices fill the chilly moist air with sweet song;
they are not quite in time and certainly fall far from the
pitch, but they are innocent and charming. Monica sees
that the trio is enchanted, and Josef might even be
touched.

Even as her mother bows prettily to the applause—
what an old pro she is!—and leads the children off the
stage, Monica's father makes his way through the
crowd to meet Irina, greeting her with a warm hug and
a kiss. Blessed Irina, wise Irina, who knew exactly what
to do! Everything is going so well!

Monica is pushing through the crowd when the band
bursts into the first bars of "O Canada," at which point
Courtney stops and stands perfectly still at attention,
patriotically singing. Apparently Irina has pointed
Monica out to her father, for he smiles at her with
recognition, and she can wait no longer but breaks
away from Courtney and rushes into her father's arms.
He kisses her, holds her, and she wants only to rest her
head on his shoulder and close her eyes in ecstasy. She
is so happy now, happy as a child, happier than she
could ever have imagined!

"How grown-up you are!" Her father whispers because people are still singing.

Don't ever leave me again, she wants to say, but
instead mumbles, "But I'm not as grown-up as you
think. Not entirely."

The song ends and speeches by the mayor and the
town clerk begin; during these Josef, with his arms
proudly around Irina and Monica, introduces them to
David Rosling, the cellist, who grins and bobs his curly
head at them in greeting, and to the pale pianist, who,
Monica realizes, is not much older than she. Monica
dislikes her immediately. "This is Melanie Burd," her
father says. Monica thinks of her as Melancholy Bird,
for she does not smile.

Courtney has joined the group and Monica introduces him, but a woman turns around to the group with
a furious "Shush," for Mrs. Heatherington is announc-

ing the big event, the crowning of the Festival Queen.

The band strikes up a march that hovers between military firmness and English music-hall vaudeville, and at the sound of this familiar queen-crowning music Monica finds a catch in her throat, for at one time she looked forward with all her heart to being the Festival Queen, and now she knows she never will be. How silly to care, especially now when her father is here. And yet she cares.

The crowd strains to see Bonnie walking grandly from the school to the platform. Two serious little girls hold up the hem of her cape so that it will not fall into the mud, and Bonnie steps carefully. Pretty but goose-pimpled in the chilly air, she is welcomed to the platform, where she stands, knees shaking with nervousness, as the purple cloak blows in the wind, exposing her in the meager white bikini that stretches over her flat tummy and tiny breasts. Last year's Queen speaks through her nose—she has a dripping cold—as she makes a speech welcoming the new Queen; then she places the crown of metal woven with flowers on Bonnie's head while someone else places a bouquet of roses in her arms. The long silky hair blows around her shoulders and Bonnie is left alone to face the audience.

In a high breathless voice, tears of excitement streaming from her eyes, she says, "This is the happiest and proudest day of my life!"

"Poor girl, I bet it is," the cellist says. A horse whinnies; the goats bleat, sending the sheep off into prolonged baaing. It's as if they were applauding the Festival Queen along with the crowd. The corners of Josef's mouth twitch slightly and dimples appear on his cheeks, as though he is too polite to laugh although he

finds this humorous. Suddenly Monica sees the crowning of the Queen and the whole Festival as slightly
ridiculous, and yet she understands that Bonnie is as
serious as if she were taking vows, and she knows that
the little girls who hold her cape may be dreaming of
the day when they will be Festival Queen. There, she is
no longer jealous of Bonnie after all, Bonnie who has
been crowned in a pasture to the bleating of goats and
has declared that this is the happiest day of her life.

It's the happiest day of Monica's life, she believes,
now that her father is here, his deep blue eyes meeting
hers, which are the same color.

"Well, Monica, you look remarkable, you know.
Quite the beauty. Are you still going to that girls'
school, what's it called?"

"Elizabeth Chatham. Yes, I'm still going there."

"I'm so pleased you earned your own scholarships. I
hear it's a wonderful school—found out from someone
who had a niece who went there. How do you like
it?"

"It's good, but stodgy, especially after Berkeley,
which I really did love. Sometimes school gets to be a
little like a convent."

"Don't let that worry you. Everyone is supposed to
complain of school. By the way, I'm sorry I couldn't
make it for that Parents' Night affair. Will you forgive
me?"

"Yes." She laughs archly. "If you promise to make
up for it . . ." She is flirting now, acting coy, lowering
her eyes and raising them, as if she weren't sure how to
behave with her father.

"We'll make up for it, don't worry about that. Tell
me, what about your music?"

"There isn't any to speak of . . . well . . ." She hesitates. There is too much to explain.

"What? You don't play anymore? You were a good little pianist."

"Was I really?" she asks, and now she is not coy anymore. The words emerge with a touch of anger, and to her horror she wants to upbraid him and demand to know why he let her go then, why he did not care about this before, when she needed him. She had not dreamed of this anger within her, and this is no time for it. Fortunately he has not caught the steely tone in her voice, and now Gabrielle dashes up to Josef and throws her arms around him.

"Daddy, Daddy, I thought you'd never come. I've been waiting and waiting and *waiting* forever!"

That little hypocrite—why, she's smarter than I am, Monica thinks, as her father, overcome at this welcome, grins at the piquant elfin face.

"So this is my little Gabrielle! Growing up! Well, well, well!" His eyes sparkle, telling her how beautiful she is. And Gabrielle *is* beautiful, that gamine in muddy shorts with the basket on her head, more bedraggled than ever with its wilting stalks of broccoli and its dried orange peel. No wonder Irina did not insist on Gabrielle's wearing a pretty dress. It is more important that she play the role of the charming waif.

"And you think horses are beautiful?" Josef asks, amused at her T-shirt. "And what is that thing on your head?"

"My salad hat. I made it for the contest but I didn't win first prize, only second." She pouts prettily.

"Why, it should have won all the prizes," her father consoles her, and David Rosling admires it although Melanie Burd seems disapproving.

It begins to sprinkle, but Irina stands tall and takes a deep breath as though this is the loveliest of spring days. Now that Josef has paid a bit of attention to each of the girls, she draws him to her once more. She chatters about hardly being able to wait to hear his beautiful violin once more and asks about the home in Berkeley, and does he remember the wonderful after-concert parties they used to have and the Sunday brunches, and is that dear lemon tree on the patio still bearing fruit? . . .

Stop, Mother, Monica is tempted to cry. She is talking too much, gushing too hard. Fortunately, the rain comes down in fat wet drops that can no longer be ignored, particularly by Josef in his suede coat.

Mrs. Heatherington's chauffeur runs over with umbrellas for the trio and announces that the great lady is ready to take them home so that they can rest before the concert. Josef heaves his shoulders in mock regret.

"You will come to the concert tonight, won't you, Irina?" he asks.

"As if we could possibly stay away . . ." Irina murmurs, her voice taking on a fruity, slightly European accent that gives a seductive quality to her speech, as she well knows. She is too obviously flirting, unaware of how silly it is while the rain pours down on everyone.

The trio runs to the limousine, but Irina stands firmly, smiling after them. She holds the white shawl over her head and stretches it to protect her daughters, who stand beside her as they shiver in the cold. Josef pauses to take a last look at his girls and blow them a kiss before he steps into the car.

No sooner does it leave when Irina clasps her hands, obviously delighted with the way things are going. Then they run to the shelter of the booth. Sheila, whom Monica has put out of her mind, comes running out in the rain to greet them, and Monica introduces her quickly to Irina and Gabrielle.

"Aunt Kathryn says I can come and stay with her, because she's all alone, and we're going to the concert tonight."

"Isn't Aunt Kathryn wonderful? You'll have a great time," Monica says.

"I came here to be with you, but I guess it's all right," Sheila says, not quite sure. Monica promises her that on Monday morning, after her father has left, they will get together and have a wonderful time, though Monica has no idea what they will do.

"It's pouring. We've got to pack up and get home!" Kathryn says. "Come along, Sheila, or you'll become liquefied out here!"

They disappear in the pelting rain, Irina locks the booth, and, with Gabrielle on one side and Monica on the other, runs home.

6

The Concert

"It's so good to be doing a concert again!" Irina cries from the steamy bathroom, where she bathes in bubbles and bath oils, the dark hair piled high on top of her head. She sings, fully a tone sharp now. Nobody would guess that she and Monica have brought home all the sweaters, scarves, and so on that were supposed to have been sold so that they could exist during the coming summer. She's counting on a different victory, Monica realizes as she piles a year of Irina's work inside the closet, out of sight.

Monica has criticized herself severely for the way in which she met her father. She shouldn't have worn those dreadful glasses or the patched skirt, which now seems to have been wrong, and she was too sharp-tongued. But she will make up for it tonight.

She loves herself in the new blue dress, has tied and untied a ribbon around her neck at least five times. Is it too sweet? Is she too old for a blue velvet ribbon? She decides to wear it anyway, for he adores pretty girls who wear pretty feminine things. She shoves the hated eyeglasses into the back of the drawer and prays that he will buy her contact lenses when she goes back to California with him. Her hair, shining with auburn lights, hangs loosely over her shoulders; a touch of blue eye shadow is enough to make her eyes sparkle. One more glance in the full-length mirror assures her that her father will find her beautiful.

And ten minutes later, as she stands at the Town Hall waiting to give out programs and show concertgoers to their seats, she is aware that she is on display and possibly admired. At least Courtney, impeccably dressed, seizes her hands and whispers in her ear, "Magnificent! Monica, you are *fantastic!*" And he would stand there forever smiling into her eyes if his mother did not pull him away, protesting that that glorious girl had work to do. She too shows clearly that

Monica surpasses herself tonight. Tom and Dennis shower her with gallantries, as she might have expected, and Kathryn, tall and unusually dignified in an embroidered Chinese coat, whispers that Monica has never looked lovelier. But it is Sheila, tagging along behind Kathryn, who stares open-mouthed at her roommate. "Wow, you're just like an actress!" she insists—the greatest praise that occurs to her—and Monica suddenly feels a rush of sympathy for her wan roommate, who is still wearing her school uniform. She determines that she *will* do something for poor Sheila, but not until later, much later.

Everyone comes. The hall is filling up. Mrs. Heatherington has a genius for selling tickets for all her projects, and besides, one must go to the concert in order to attend the traditional square dance that will be held afterward. Monica hopes that her father does not know this, for it would hurt his vanity.

The concert is held up until the Festival Committee arrives, and now Monica leads the procession to their reserved seats in the front row. Mrs. Heatherington's dress is splashed with cabbage roses and she nods imperiously to the members of the audience as the mayor leads her to her seat. Three other members, ridiculously overdressed, follow; and at last Irina comes, slightly apart from the others, and all eyes are on her.

Never has she looked more exquisite, more the countess. Her hair is carefully arranged high on her head except for the two curls that flirt on her cheeks; her eyes blaze; the crystal pendant and earrings glitter and swing as she walks proudly, a lacy mohair stole dropped carelessly over her arm as though this were a languorous summer night instead of a chilly Genessee evening. As Monica shows her to her seat, she winks subtly, as if this coup they are planning can turn out only victoriously.

The hubbub of talk quiets as the spotlights are turned toward the stage and the lights in the hall, which cannot be dimmed, are simply turned out. Standing at the rear of the hall, Monica is aware of a sudden lurch of her stomach, the old stage fright coming back, as though she herself were expected to walk onto the stage, bow, sit at the piano, and perform. She is nearly ill with panic.

Yet the trio walks onstage confidently. Her father bows deeply, professionally. In contrast, David Rosling seems very young and informal. But it is the girl who is all wrong, not the least bit exciting. Her straight mouse-colored hair is pulled back and held with a barrette at the nape of her long neck, and her dress is a sober, unimaginative long-skirted shirtwaist. Monica wonders that her father, who always used to manage to find pianists who were as lovely as they were competent, should have settled on this plain "Melancholy Bird."

Yet Monica is to be surprised. The Bird comes alive in the opening Haydn trio; she plays well, very well indeed, and her vitality completes the warmth and rich-ness of the strings. It's been so long since she has heard live music that Monica is overwhelmed with the ele-gance of the sound and cannot drink it in fast enough. The trio plays superbly, with perfect tone and perfect balance. The theme travels from one player to another; it's like an exquisite game of catch.

"If only I were a musician . . ." The phrase catches in her throat. Her father used to tell her that there was nothing more important in all the world than music, and now she knows that for him this is true. And for herself? It could have been true, but it's too late now. Too late!

The trio now plays the "Archduke Trio," and she remembers the first time she heard it, a treasure buried and nearly forgotten.

> *She is a child of six, curled in a large chair upholstered in ancient brocade, in the heavily furnished living room of an apartment in Rome. It was once a section of a* palazzo, *and the cherubs painted on the ceiling, though faded, still smile down playfully at her. She sees clearly the bowl of fruit on the inlaid coffee table and a sheet of music left there—it is as brilliant as a still life. But it is the sound from the music room that flows over her, the richness of the cello and the constant movement of the piano and the bravery of the violin that holds her, suspends her in time.*
>
> *When she grows up, she promises herself, she will play this music.*

Here is it almost ten years later, and she doesn't play the piano at all. During the intermission she stands alone in the dark outside the concert hall and weeps.

But when she returns for the second part of the program, she is composed. Her father has promised Mrs. Heatherington a solo, and he has chosen the Franck Sonata in A major. That is for her, Monica knows, for shortly before leaving California she had "discovered" and fallen in love with that music, and this had pleased him. Now, as he lifts his violin to his chin, Monica

senses that his eyes are scanning the hall to reach hers.
The flowing theme begins—moody questions without
answers. The Bird stretches her long neck over the
piano keys and plays fearlessly and delicately so that
the sensitive shading of the violin may be heard. When
did she hear this last? Only one week, or was it slightly
more, before they left La Californie? That too she had
forgotten all this time.

> *It was a Sunday afternoon, when all of the
> guests had left after one of Irina's celebrated
> brunches, and Monica had settled down to her
> homework in the far corner of the living room. An
> argument escalated in the kitchen. She covered her
> ears, yet still could not help but hear Irina's
> screaming accusations and Josef's low but vicious
> replies, followed by the smashing of dishes against
> the wall and the harsh crack of Josef slapping his
> wife's face and her cries—all of this suddenly si-
> lenced by the ring of the doorbell. It was Josef's
> accompanist, the bald-headed Mr. Fielding, over
> whom nobody could be jealous, coming to re-
> hearse for a concert.*
>
> *Monica, quivering from her parents' quarrel,
> could not study, could not think. And then the
> music began, the Franck sonata with its plaintive
> melody, its storms, and finally its lyrical sweep—a
> sense of hope tinged with sadness.*
>
> *"This music is myself," she had discovered then
> and been comforted.*

And now as her father's full tones sweep through the
hall, she is nearly healed again. Her father is speaking

to her with his violin, and he says, "It is all right, Monica; you see, I do understand you." And she wants to tell him, "I love you, Father, and I will never love anyone else in the same way, not ever."

The trio returns to play, to bow, to give two encores. A victory!

Monica longs to rush backstage as she did so many times as a child, when he would pick her up and kiss her and his love would flow around her. Then would follow the little ceremony in which she would kiss his violin before he wrapped it in its silk scarf and locked it in its case. Too old for that now, she stands outside the dressing-room door while the trio is being praised, gushed over, and admired. At last Josef catches sight of Monica, cuts through the crowd, and takes her in his arms, understanding that she is too full of emotions to speak. Then he releases her.

"Monica, you'll be at the reception, the dance or whatever it is, won't you? Wait for me there, dear. I want to speak to you!" he says, patting her cheek. Gratified, she whispers yes and leaves.

————7

Ending on an Upbeat

The dance has been set up in another hall, a converted barn across the street. The atmosphere is hardly that of the concert hall. The local dance band—i.e., fiddler, accordionist, electric guitarist, and drummer—are setting up their instruments. The hushed chatting of the concert hall has given way to a louder and more relaxed babble of talk. Sheila follows Monica, chatting all the while about the beautiful concert, and begs Monica to let her stand behind the refreshment table to serve cider, coffee, and doughnuts. This is one of Monica's duties, and graciously she lets Sheila help.

Irina walks in with the trio, and she appears so triumphant that one might think she too had performed. She leads them to the refreshment table and Monica serves them. Josef and Irina stand near enough so that she overhears them.

"Irina, love, I can't get over the way you look. How do you manage to keep so young? This Island must be agreeing with you."

"It's not the Island, Josef. It's that remarkable concert. You are superb! You play more beautifully than ever. My fingers and toes tingle just the way they used to whenever you played."

"And the rest of the trio, didn't you like them?"

"Loved you all! Perfect ensemble."

"It's the beautiful lady in the front row who helped us play well."

Irina throws back her head and laughs delightedly. What a ham she is, Monica thinks. And her father is just as bad. They are playing a familiar game; it's a kind of vaudeville routine in which each tries to top the other's compliment. Monica knows how these tournaments end: the pace quickens so that they are practically shouting compliments at each other with a kind of "Take that!" and "You take that!" attitude. As for the other side of the coin, the real fights . . .

But she must live in the present, now, tonight! See

how well everything is going, Monica, how your mother flirts with your father and how he is paying extravagant compliments to her.

"They're really going at it, aren't they?" David Rosling asks, as he stands beside Monica and sips cider. "Looks like a fertility rite from here."

She giggles. "Just an old vaudeville routine."

David seems about to say something more, then checks it, whatever it may be. "Did you like the concert, Monica?"

She places a hand on his sleeve. "I haven't even congratulated you yet! It was great. I loved it, really loved it. You are a terrific cellist, but of course you know that."

"I'm not always that sure. Was I too loud, do you think?"

"Not at all. The balance was perfect. Do you like being in a trio?"

"Sure. I'd like to be a soloist, of course, but I'm grateful to your father for letting me play. It's like having a roof over my head for a while. I've been pretty much the wanderer."

"My father was a gypsy for a long time. Concert tours. We were never in one place long enough to call it home—not until we got to Berkeley."

"Wandering is okay. I'd never have found this island otherwise. Such a remarkable place! You must be crazy about it."

"Well, I am, and then again I'm not. I'm ready to move."

"Really! Say, aren't you some kind of musician? A pianist, I think your father said."

"Did he really say that? What did he say actually?"

She betrays herself, wanting to know too much. A familiar pain returns, a constriction in her throat. "Actually, I don't play anymore."

She smiles falsely, even giggles a bit, because she doesn't want to think of this failure anymore. Fortunately, Courtney saves the conversation by coming up.

"Monica, a terrific concert! Your father's *all right*. And Mr. Rosling, you're terrific too. Welcome to the Island."

"Thanks very much."

"Hope they start the dancing soon. Monica, I've been looking forward to this. I'm afraid, Mr. Rosling, you're not going to be exactly crazy about the local band. Typically Island, I'm afraid."

David mumbles something about its being quite perfect. The band in fact is tuning up, loudly and amateurishly. The jazzed-up shirts, assortment of hats, and self-conscious gesturing are, as Courtney puts it, strictly Island. Monica sees her mother talking with Mr. Dayton, the caller, and feels a shiver of apprehension. And sure enough, after the first brief square dance, which Monica performs with Courtney, the caller announces that in honor of the concert artists, they will play a series of polkas. "Now we aren't exactly used to it, but if you'll all join in, you'll catch on!"

David grins as Irina and Josef take their places. "I've got to see this. I've never seen Josef dance."

"He's good. He used to be good, anyway," Monica says defensively, and she crosses her fingers as the dance begins and she watches.

With relief she sees that Josef and Irina perform with the same elegance and grace that always came so naturally to them. They continue to dance even after the others have become winded and have retired to the sides, and finally they are the only ones on the floor, ending the series of polkas with a sentimental waltz. Irina throws her head back and smiles broadly as though she were onstage, and Josef, though somewhat out of breath, twirls her around and does not lose a beat. The audience applauds in time to the music and, grinning, David cries to Monica, "It's a marathon and they've won!" Finally the dance is over and Josef and Irina, breathing hard and holding their sides, walk over to the chairs and sit down gratefully.

"That mother of yours is the greatest!" Courtney says, his eyes wide with admiration. Monica accepts the compliment, but suddenly wishes she did not have to applaud her parents all the time. Should it not be the other way around?

Another dance begins, a country dance that everyone knows, and Courtney takes it for granted that Monica will dance with him, but instead David Rosling leads Monica to the floor. Courtney is left behind looking puzzled. David dances well, and now Monica senses that Josef and Irina, who may still be a little short of breath, are watching her. Her cheeks are flushed; her eyes flash with light and she feels drunk, although she has not even so much as sipped the cider. Everything is going so well!

She dances with David, then with Courtney, and now her father cuts in, insists on dancing with his daughter. He moves with a certain old-fashioned courtliness and holds her gaze with his eyes. At the end of the dance they linger at the far end of the hall.

"You've grown up so fast, little Monica, and I wasn't even there to see it."

"I'm not completely grown yet; at least, I have one more year of high school. Please, Dad, will you take me back to California with you?"

"Monica, I would love to!"

"Then, will you? Please, will you take me back? I'll study hard. I'll even study piano again if you want me to. I'll take care of you. I just want to be with you."

"But darling, there's the trio. Really, I'm never home. We are booked up for many concerts, and that means traveling. When I'm at home, there are always classes, rehearsals, appearances. You're better off with your mother, or going to that remarkable school."

"Mother would go back too. Everything would be beautiful . . ."

"I'll think about it . . ." he promises, and then he is relieved by Mrs. Heatherington, who apologizes to Monica as she leads Josef away to meet somebody. In the meantime, David is dancing with the Bird and Courtney is chatting with Kathryn and Sheila. Gabrielle, who has been dressed for the night's occasion as the charming and proper daughter of a great musician, has had too much of the cider, which is actually quite hard, and she is racing around wildly with some of the ten-year-old Island boys. Monica glowers at her and wishes Irina would take better care of her.

"Dance with me!" David begs as he glides over to her before the start of the next square dance, and at the same time Courtney dashes across the floor to her. What a happy situation, to have David and Courtney glower at each other! "David got here first, but afterward I'll dance with you," she tells Courtney.

However, before two dances have passed, leaving Monica breathless and whirling, Irina comes over to beg her to take Gabrielle home. "She's getting overtired and we don't want Josef to see that she isn't quite the perfect child, not when everything is going so well. He's crazy about *you*, Monica! I'll be home a little later," she says.

"Mother, I can't go now," she whispers desperately. David is waiting to dance with her, and it's clear that Courtney too is about to claim a dance. "This is no time to leave. Why do I have to look after Gabrielle? Anyway, she's not all that bad."

Irina's eyes harden for a moment, then soften as she gives in. "All right, Monica, one more dance—only one! And then will you take her home, please? Everything that happens is important, very important. You know that."

"I suppose," Monica answers gracelessly, and Irina leaves.

"I can take you home if you'll let me," Courtney says.

"After she dances with me," David Rosling insists as he takes Monica's hand and leads her to the floor.

"Thanks, Courtney, I'd love it, even if I have to drag Gabrielle."

David Rosling looks down at Monica as they dance and a tender smile plays around his lips. "I never dreamed old Josef had such a charming daughter. I hope I'll be seeing you again, Monica."

"I hope so too. It's great to meet you, to meet such a grand cellist *and* good dancer. You didn't step on my toes once!"

"Sheer luck!" he says. When the dance is over, he kisses her hand and lets her go. At that very point Sheila rushes up.

"Didja see me dance, Monica? I'm having the best time . . ."

"That's good." Apparently one of the local high school boys asked her to dance, and this made her evening perfect.

"I have to go," Sheila complains lightly—Kathryn is waiting at the door.

"I have to go too and put Gabrielle to bed," Monica assures her so she won't feel deprived. Sheila waves a coy good-bye to Courtney and leaves.

As she might have expected, Gabrielle attempts to wiggle out of Monica's grasp until Monica bribes her with the promise of hot chocolate and a story.

"And if that doesn't work, I shall think of something wicked to do to you," Courtney jokes in mock sternness, and Gabrielle giggles. As Monica walks with Courtney to the door, she sees that her father is dancing with Melanie Burd, and something about this is disquieting, yet she shrugs it off with an explanation that he must feel obliged to do so.

Gabrielle is slightly drunk and Courtney knows exactly what to say to make her giggle and become compliant enough to let him carry her piggyback up the stairs to her bed. He whispers that if Gabrielle will get herself tucked into her bed, Monica will bring her a tray of delights and tell her a story.

"She's not so difficult," he says to Monica as he comes down the stairs.

"But she's not *your* sister." Monica laughs. "Oh Courtney, I'm so grateful to you. You always know just what to do."

"Like finding a minute to kiss you?" he says, drawing her close to him and holding her. "Your hair is so fragrant, your eyes are so shining . . . oh Monica, Monica!"

They cling to each other. How sweet is is to be in his arms! They peer into each other's eyes, then kiss again until they hear Gabrielle calling.

"I'm waiting!" she insists. It breaks the spell.

"Good night, dear Monica. Don't forget, you're having dinner with us tomorrow. Come early, as early as you can make it, okay?"

"Yes, I will—as soon as I can get away," she whispers, and he leaves.

Dutifully, dreamily, she listens to Gabrielle's prattle, gives her hot chocolate, tells her a brief story, and covers her as she kisses her good night.

Then Monica undresses, climbs into bed—and finds that she cannot sleep. Her father has not said yes to her request, but he has not refused either. The birds have already begun their morning chorus when she falls exhausted into a sweet-dreaming sleep.

PART FOUR

A Significant Sunday

1
The Promise

Now that the Festival is over, the sun shines victoriously in a vast cerulean sky and the white clouds puff around it to celebrate the day. The morning sings with sunlight, webs on the grass scintillate with points of light, and birds trill from the lilac bushes, the maples, and the cedars. A rooster crows triumphantly and will not be put down. A flock of pigeons fling themselves into the sky, where they wheel with exuberance.

"It's a promise," Monica believes as she stands at the dormer window. Ordinarily she has little patience with superstition, yet now she sees symbols everywhere, as she did yesterday. The sun shines after the gloomy rains because her life is about to begin a new, sun-filled phase. Happiness wells up inside her; she is ready to love everyone, and cannot stay in bed, but must go downstairs to share this vibrant joy.

She nearly collides with her mother, who is coming from the back porch into the kitchen with an immense glass bowl in her arms, the familiar bowl that will soon be filled with a glowing mosaic of fruit. Radiant Irina, she too feels the promise of the day. Monica takes the bowl from her, sets it on the table, and then hugs Irina.

They share a remarkable secret, this inspired conspiracy.

"You were gorgeous last night, Mother. You and Dad were the hit of the dance."

"Really, Monica? Do you think we looked all right? I felt a little self-conscious when we were the *only* ones on the floor."

Monica does not believe this, of course, not for a second, for Irina loves nothing more than to be the center of attention, and even now she smiles such a pleased catlike smile that it's clear that embarrassment is the least likely reaction Irina would ever have to any situation. She is still glowing as she pours hot fragrant coffee into the two china cups she has set on the breakfast table.

"I guess Daddy didn't come back with you last night then, did he?" Monica asks, speaking softly, for this may be a tender matter for Irina.

"He certainly wanted to, I'm quite sure, but dear old Mrs. H. saw to it that he slept at her castle. After all, this is a small island. It's like any small town. People talk."

Since when have "people talking" ever bothered her mother? Since when has her father been intimidated by Mrs. Heatherington or anyone else?

"That's pretty silly, Mother. Nobody even thinks about things like that anymore."

"Ooooh, yes they do, pet. People *talk*. It's hilarious to think that Josef and I would have to sneak off to be together, just as if we weren't married."

"Mother, you *aren't* married," Monica says firmly, immediately sorry for being so blunt, and also frightened. How can her mother forget the fact of divorce so easily? How can she pretend it never happened? Irina's eyes lower and she stops drinking her coffee. Monica understands that her mother can sink into a depression that lies just below the surface of her good spirits, and it would never do for Irina to play the role of the gloomy fatalist now. She cheers her with praise.

"David Rosling just couldn't *believe* how attractive you and Daddy are when you dance. It made me very proud of you." There, this makes her mother feel better. A smile drifts over her face.

"Right from the very beginning, Josef and I could dance together. We are absolutely perfect for each other—in dancing and in other ways too. No other man has ever been so good for me. I hope that he sees that now."

"I do too," Monica says, pleading that this will be so. "What time will he get here?"

"About ten-fifteen. He likes to sleep late, you know. It will be just the four of us, one perfect little family. This is why he accepted the invitation here, to this out-of-the-way place—just to see us."

"Do you really believe that, Mother? He's being paid a lot for this concert, and he may even think of it as a kind of vacation."

"What's the matter with you, Monica? He's here to see *us*. He was delighted to see us; couldn't you tell? About the money, well, I cannot fool myself. I know Josef's weaknesses as well as his strong points. He simply can't turn down money, and that's the truth. And he has a way of flattering people; he sticks his words together with jam and whipped cream. Still, I'm sure he was glad to see us. Besides, my horoscope in the *Genessee Journal* looks very good."

"You believe the *Journal's* horoscope? Good Lord, Mother." Monica chides her mother for being superstitious, and yet she herself has been seeing signs and portents everywhere.

"Here, taste this. Tell me I haven't lost my touch with pastry," Irina says as she takes two cheese buns from the oven.

Monica tastes the flaky Danish. "If nothing else will get Daddy back, Mom, this should! It's so sinful, so good, and I'll get so fat if I eat any more of it! When it comes to pastry, you *are* a genius if ever I've seen one."

"Think so?" Irina thrives on praise, which she truly deserves in this instance. It occurs to Monica that she has a tremendous need to be loved, a greater need than almost anyone Monica has ever known. How odd it is that Irina, her mother, can sometimes act as though she were Monica's child!

Irina nibbles the crust of her bun but does not eat, does not finish her coffee. She has prepared endless pastries for the occasion, everything that Josef has ever loved: buns, butter rolls, poppy-seed squares, and blueberry tarts—enough to feed twenty people. Monica knows that because of this and all the other luxuries her mother has bought for the occasion, they will have to live on leftovers for the rest of the month. And yet the grand gesture, going all the way, is in the very nature of her mother.

"Monica, it's getting late. We'd better begin!" Irina cries, springing up to clear the table. "I'd better get the flowers out of the way first."

While Irina arranges the lilacs, forsythia, and bridal veil, Monica senses the vibrations of the coming party. What a happy excitement and a certain urgency to clean and straighten the house and then take from the refrigerator all those fine things to eat, arranging them on plates, seeing that everything will be perfect! Louka is already twitching her tail and watching, eyes big and green and begging as she senses the good things that will be coming.

"Remember how it used to be, darling?" Irina asks absently.

Monica remembers well, but it was different then. There was always so much music in the house, long before the guests came for brunch, and the telephone never stopped ringing. She can even hear her father's genial voice as he says, "Sure, come along, and please bring your friend! Yes, of course, it's all right!" And then Monica would have to set an extra place or two for this interesting bassoon player who would be along or his girlfriend who studied astrology or that visiting Irish poet who could easily be coaxed into reciting his verse. On sunny mornings the bougainvillea sparkled and its leaves dappled the table on the patio with delicate shadows. There was a hubbub of talk, endless talk, toasts to Irina, bursts of laughter, and always someone getting up from the table to sing or demonstrate a certain musical point on a flute or cello. It was a small theater in its way, with people forever coming and going.

But this house is quiet.

In the morning light Monica sees that this house in Genessee is dusty; in Berkeley there was always a live-in student who took care of that. Irina is hardly the perfect housekeeper, yet she loves to keep her house and does not care that there's dust, but insists that this red cushion should be placed on the floor, at exactly this location—and if the sunlight streams through the stained-glass window to drench the opposite wall, with color, then it hardly matters that a spider has chosen to spin a web there. It is Monica who dusts, cleans, sweeps, and removes the spider by carefully putting him in a spot outdoors where she hopes he belongs.

"What's this spinning wheel doing here, and this basket of carded wool?" she asks Irina, who is not a weaver. Yet the spinning wheel adds a quaint homey touch, suggesting old-fashioned virtues of thrift and hard work.

"I just borrowed it for a few days, dear. Think it looks nice?"

Borrow, lend, borrow, lend. It is Irina's belief that possessions are meant to be moved from one place to another. It embarrasses Monica that her mother thinks nothing of borrowing shamelessly, and yet she does give of herself readily without expecting to be repaid. She dyes a friend's hair; boards dogs, cats, and children when they have no other place to go; finishes sewing a dress that a neighbor has begun and cannot bear to finish. Clothes and objects flow to the house and from it as well. Life is fluid; it must move, never become stationary, never stay in the same place.

Perhaps this is why her mother is never defeated. For all her worldly failures—the ballet, the painting, the marriage, the teaching, and now perhaps her shop—she is unconquered. As long as there is movement, there is change and there is hope! Yet what a contradictory person she is after all, needing to go from one thing to another and yet longing to be settled, longing to take root in a comfortable suburban home. How can anyone understand Irina? She is so many different people.

"Do you like this tablecloth?" Irina asks as Monica helps her place the pale linen cloth over the round table. "It's a second, but I'll bet you can't even tell where I mended it, can you?"

"Mom, don't talk about your bargains. Dad hates it and so do I."

Irina stops short, hurt. "I was only trying to teach you something about purchasing. It's something I know how to do."

"I know, Mom. I'm sorry, but it's true—Daddy doesn't like to hear about it."

"But I'm not telling *him*. Darling, do you think I don't know him thoroughly, what he likes and what annoys him? I'm only telling you because someday you'll want a lovely home. Now, see this Danish bowl? I didn't pay for it. I crocheted a sweater and took this in payment. I want you to know that if you use your head you can trade, you can find out how to buy things, and it's a game. Really, that's what it is. And it's worth it, if you like lovely things."

As she says this she holds a Royal Danish blue and white plate up to the light, she can see her fingers through it. There may not be enough food to last out the week, but they will have fine dishes even if they must resort to eating boiled dandelion greens.

"I think we're different from other people. It's so funny . . ." Monica's voice drifts. She is thinking of Courtney's mother, who could certainly buy all the exquisite china anyone could wish, yet uses cheap, heavy pottery from a supermarket because, after all, "Skiffington is only a summer place." She cannot delight in bargains, because she doesn't *need* bargains. Why does she seem to lack a certain zest for living, then, compared to Irina? In this light, Irina becomes infinitely more interesting. How odd that she did not see this before!

All this talk of table linen, pottery, and purchasing, so unexpected at a time like this, is a ploy to hide the nervousness they feel.

"I'm glad that you're my mother, do you know that?" Monica asks Irina, who is now preparing layers of strawberries sliced and sugared in a cut-glass bowl.

"You like me, then? And you like your father too? How convenient!"

"It's because you and Dad are both touched. Daft. Weird. And not like anyone else." Especially not like Courtney's mother, who could never dream of accenting a bowl of strawberries with the purple blue of berries frozen the summer before.

"There!" Irina holds up the bowl as though a work of art has just been completed.

But time is flying. Monica peels the hard-boiled eggs and slices them, places them on thin diamonds of black bread; each yellow moon is covered with a rolled anchovy, to be grilled under the broiler. Jams of translucent apricot and crimson plum must be placed in silver jam pots and set on the table. Baskets with linen napkins are placed on the counter, ready for the cheese buns and pastries that must be heated in the oven before serving. The platter of smoked meats and cheeses, an earthenware pot of caviar, a bowl of black olives, a pitcher of cream, and a bowl of sugar are set on the table. A round pat of yellow butter with a sprig of parsley sets off the lavender of a huge bowl of lilacs. Monica and Irina stand before the table and admire it.

"It's like a Matisse," Irina says, the highest praise possible where she is concerned.

Monica thinks it looks more like a Bonnard, but this is no time to quibble. She is seized by an irrational fear—can it be that everything is too perfect?

"Mother, don't expect too much, okay? It's been a long time. People change."

"Don't worry, little one. The more they change, the more they stay the same. It will all work out," Irina assures her.

"Sure, sure, of course it will," Monica says with conviction. Damn, it simply *can't* fail now, after all this work.

Gabrielle appears in her pajamas. She yawns, rubs her eyes, and scratches her stomach. "What time is it? Is Daddy coming?"

"Good lord, it's ten o'clock!" Irina shrieks. "We've all got to get dressed. *Now.* Just think, he'll be here any minute!"

———2

Breakfast at Bittersweet

Ten o'clock passes. Ten-fifteen. Ten-thirty. Ten-forty. Irina and her girls stand in the living room and wait. Everything is ready; there is nothing more to do. "Like a Chekhov play," Monica comments, but Irina does not hear. Lilacs fill the house with the scent of spring, and Irina is an extension of the lilacs, delicate in a flattering violet skirt she has borrowed from one of the actresses and a lavender shirt that is too gauzy and thin for the crispness of the morning. A thin scarlet necklace accents the fragility of the outfit, and her paleness under the makeup. She fusses with a huge emerald ring as she makes excuses for Josef.

"He loves to sleep late." And five minutes later:

"Mrs. H. is probably keeping him, the old dragon." And finally:

"No wonder he's not here. Our clocks are always so fast!"

At this, Gabrielle sighs audibly and bounces upstairs. She is dressed—actually, overdressed—in a puffy white blouse and red vest and skirt that together resemble an Austrian peasant costume. "I suppose I wear a costume too," Monica muses wryly. "As if I were a native of Berkeley." But she sees the longish corduroy skirt, the boots, and the blue jersey topped by a Mexican shirt as conventional enough to balance Irina and Gabrielle's romantic dress.

"And what good will any of it be if he doesn't come?" she asks herself. Waiting is surely the worst part of all. She thinks of waiting rooms in dentists' offices and the wings of a stage where one stands before performing. Better to shut her eyes and meditate, drawing deep slow breaths—but even so she fails to shut out the dreadful possibility that he might not show up.

Then Gabrielle shouts the news from the top of the stairs.

"They're coming. The car's on its way!"

Within two minutes the limousine stops in front of Bittersweet Place and Monica's father gets out, but instead of coming up the walk directly, he waits while Melanie Burd emerges into the sunlight, followed by David Rosling.

"Oh no!" Irina groans in dismay. "Did he *have* to bring them?"

"How can he be so dense!" Monica cries, yet she cannot suppress a certain unexpected delight at seeing David Rosling again.

"I made it so clear that it would just be us," Irina says; then, immediately forgiving Josef, continues. "Well, he's like that, generous, impulsive. Always bringing someone home."

Monica goes to the kitchen to find plates with which to set two extra places at the table and hears Irina greeting the guests. She has recovered quickly, but Monica detects a fluttering in her voice.

"How nice you could come! See what a fine day we've come up with to make up for yesterday?"

As Monica takes care of last-minute preparations in the kitchen, she peeks into the living room from time to time and hears snatches of conversation.

Irina chatters and chatters and it doesn't matter what she says so long as a terrible silence doesn't fall on the party. Josef has his arm around Gabrielle as he looks around, and David Rosling is appreciating everything—his charming hostess, the sunshine, the Island, this delightful house. "You must be so happy here, Irina. No traffic, no smog. I'll bet you can even go out walking at night without fear of being mugged. And all this marvelous fresh air!" He breathes it in deeply as if it were ambrosia.

The Melancholy Bird, a brown wren in a dull-hued pantsuit, murmurs something polite, and when Irina invites her to sit down, perches like an obedient child on the edge of a chair.

Irina's voice floats but does not say much of anything. So far the conversation is the usual party talk of unfinished sentences, murmurings, vague phrases. Monica wants to greet her father, yet hesitates. He walks around the room, judging it, peering at an etching on the wall, regarding one of Kathryn's pots, touching the spinning wheel appreciatively, and picking up a piece of carded wool, which he shows to Melanie, asking her to feel how soft it is.

"Well, Irina, I guess you're keeping yourself busy. Into all sorts of things, eh?"

Irina's face clouds, for she does not like what she takes seriously to be passed off as a hobby, something to while the time away. Does Josef know this? At any rate, now is the time for Monica to make an entrance and head off a tiff. She strides into the living room.

"Hello, Daddy!"

She has rehearsed this so often, that it is like a part in a play. Josef knows his role and turns toward her with his eyes genuinely lit with pleasure, kissing her in a fatherly way. What marvelous cologne he uses!

"Irina, where did we ever find such a beauty? And why did you let her grow up so fast? Why, when I saw her last, she was . . ." He shakes his head to indicate how tiny she was, and one would think by his gesture that she had been only five or six years old, when in fact she had been twelve and hardly a little girl. Let it pass! He sits on the sofa and draws her down beside him.

"Now we can talk. I'm such a lucky man with these wonderful girls!" he says, although his eyes are for Monica alone. How hopeful this seems! "Now tell me, Monica, do the boys chase you day and night?"

"No, no, no!" she says, shaking her head with mock seriousness. "Don't forget, the school I go to is practically a convent, if you want to see it that way."

"It's a superb school, I understand. Tell me, what goes on there in the way of music? Or have you found something else more intriguing?"

"Well, Chatham's an experience, I guess," Monica says, treading a narrow path, for she does not want to appear difficult to please, and yet she would like her father to know she is ready for something more realistic, such as the public school in Berkeley. The conversation falters, and he changes the subject.

"Remind me to get a picture of you; I want three photos, Monica—one for my office, one for home, and one for my pocket. I want to show you off."

"Why bother with photographs when you could just pack me up and take me along with you?" she says with a little laugh at this daring proposal. Can he guess how she longs for him to take her up on it? But he just smiles broadly, pats her cheek, and avoids answering.

"What a sweet girl, and a smart girl too! David, can you guess how many thousands of dollars' worth of scholarships she's won? Remarkable!"

Monica smiles patiently. It's what Irina would call Josef's whipped cream and jam—the sweetness that avoids a straight answer. But Monica stays with the issue.

"I've been dreaming about Berkeley a lot, Dad," she says. "Chatham is a fine school with lots of tradition, but it's awfully nineteenth-century, if you know what I mean. Berkeley is so alive, so alert, so with it! And of course, there's everything else. If only you knew how I missed the music and the concerts . . . how I miss hearing your violin!"

"What a sweet thing to say! I'm touched, my dear. Of course, Berkeley is a superb place, but not quite what it was when you left it. I would say that most of your friends are off to private schools, schools probably very much like the one you go to, so there'd be little advantage in going back."

This makes it sound as if a rejection is coming, so Irina averts it by interrupting: "Tell us all about the trio, Josef, and how you happened to get started. My goodness, you all get such fabulous reviews! You must have a heavy schedule?"

Josef, never at a loss when he discusses his successes, comes close to boasting about the trio's impressive concert schedule. They will spend the summer in residence somewhere in Massachusetts; they will appear at festivals throughout Europe, and there is even a projected appearance in Tokyo next fall. Irina clasps her hands theatrically.

"I've always *wanted* to go to Tokyo! And I must say, I dream of returning to Europe! It's been years since I've been anywhere. Remember what fun we used to have, Josef?"

"Fun? Traveling is an agony these days. Delays at airports, reservations—and the inflation, unbelievable! You wouldn't like it at all, Irina. Besides, you have heaven right here. As we came here on that ferry, *The Genessee Queen* . . . what a lovely name . . . and as we plowed through those cool blue waters, all I could think of was Sibelius. Something cool and northern and mystical. Don't you think so, Melanie?"

She nods in agreement.

"Josef, you're an incurable romantic," David Rosling says. "But I must admit, the same thought occurred to me. What about you, Monica, what do you think? Does it suggest music to you?"

"Something more contemporary," she says, "something electronic, but I hadn't really thought of it in just that way." She laughs nervously.

"Isn't it time we all had something to eat?" Irina says demurely, and David Rosling springs up immediately.

"I thought you'd never ask! And all those marvelous fragrances coming out of the kitchen ever since we've been here! Mmmm!"

He bends over and kisses her hand and this lightens the air, makes the gathering a party. Josef is pleased, says little; and it seems to Monica that he is not so much company but has taken over the house as his own; in some way he has become the host. What a good sign!

"Look at that table!" he cries, but then he has become a guest once more. "Beautiful, Irina, beautiful enough to be preserved in amber. I knew you wouldn't fail me. Only Irina can produce such a handsome feast."

Melanie Burd says something for the first time.

"Do you know there is a cat on your table?" she asks, obviously horrified, though she controls her voice. Of course we know, Monica thinks, as everyone watches Louka, who has just leaped onto the table and snatched a kipper and now stands there defiantly. Melanie is disgusted; Josef, perfectly mannered, appears not to have noticed anything; and David, highly amused, laughs.

"She always eats with us because she is our baby," Gabrielle explains to Melanie, who doesn't want to hear about it. Monica picks up Louka without scolding her and calmly places her in the laundry room and shuts the door.

"Please sit down, everyone!" Irina says while Gabrielle explains to Melanie that Louka took only one kipper and there are lots left. "Sit anywhere you like," Irina says, but quietly manages the seating so that Josef takes a chair beside her.

"I had to bring along Melanie and David," he says, "because I've told them so much about your brunches that they simply had to see one. Very talented, isn't she?"

"It's very nice," the Bird admits.

"Nice! Is that all you can say? It's a jewel. If I had my camera with me, I would make a study of this table," David says.

"While everything got cold?" Josef interrupts. "Now then, if we were drinking, I'd suggest a toast to Irina. That she lives so civilly on this wild island is at least a miracle. To Irina and to the Island!" He holds up a glass of pomegranate juice. "To Irina and the Island!" he repeats.

"Not that toast, Josef, please!" Irina objects. "I mean, don't have any illusions about this place. The truth is that I'm really perishing here. You know me, Josef. I'm a city person, and so homesick. I dream of Paris, Nice, London, Berkeley . . ." She finishes with an effective sigh.

"How could anyone want to leave this place?" David

Rosling asks. "It's such a heaven, I almost want to move here. Of course, I don't suppose there's a delicatessen around the corner, or foreign movies, or concerts most of the time. But Vancouver's not far, is it?"

"It's a long ride," Irina says. "One can't always get away. But you see, David, it's not simply the galleries and concerts that I miss, but the sight of people on the streets, the sound of different voices, the shops, and that wonderful feeling that so many lives are going on and so many things are happening all the time! You can't begin to know how I miss it!"

Calm down, Mother, Monica wants to say. Two red spots are burning in Irina's cheeks, and her voice is becoming too dramatic. Josef listens patiently and he must know by this time that both Monica and Irina want to return to Berkeley. It is time to play it more lightly.

"How about some cheese? We found some Boursin, and here's some choice Camembert," Monica says, jumping up and moving around with the platter. "Miss Burd, you're not taking anything. Is something wrong?"

"Everything is very nice, thank you," she replies stiffly, without looking at Monica. On her plate is an end slice of salami, half a sliver of cheese; she nibbles at a roll, sips the coffee, and follows it with cold water. Monica suspects that Melanie did not really wish to come, that the sight of Louka on the table has upset her, and that she cannot know that her refusal to eat anything is something Irina will regard as an insult. David makes up for the finicky guest by piling his plate.

"Irina," Josef says in considered tones, "it would seem to me that this island throbs with another kind of life. That Festival was charming, like something out of

Shakespeare; that dance last night was charming; and perhaps this island will become a kind of art center, a culture center. It would be a mistake to give up all this for any city."

"If you lived here, Josef, you would not find it so charming," Irina replies.

"The bulletin boards were full of notices for classes in folk dancing, bridge, weaving, real estate, dog training, the raising of goats. Whatever. Good heavens, the things that go on here!" David says.

"It so happens that I am not fascinated by classes in dog-training or bridge or raising goats," Irina says. "Let me tell you about the Island. Some of the people here are natives, farmers or fishermen or small businessmen, and the Island is all that they know. But many people come to get away from the city, to be alone for a while, or to solve problems; that's very good. But only for a certain length of time. If you stay on too long, it's a mistake, because then the Island can hound you, like any other place."

"You don't look in the least hounded, Irina," Josef says. "You've got your shop and you teach folk dancing, singing, ballet—Heaven knows what! And you're very popular, you're on all kinds of committees. Mrs. Heatherington says she doesn't know how the Island would get along without you."

Oh, blow Mrs. Heatherington, Monica thinks. Is it possible that her father doesn't know how badly everything is going, that the shop must close down at the end of summer, and that they have no income? But he *must* know, for this is the kind of information that Josef cleverly worms out of anyone, and surely he would not take Mrs. Heatherington's flattery too seriously. He also knows that Irina is a city person and that she has practically told him the truth—that she must leave this island. Why, then, does he continue to bait her? Monica suspects that nothing is going as well as it should. The conversation limps, then comes to a deadlock, which is just as well, for Irina is on the verge of begging Josef outright to rescue her, and Josef, if faced directly at this point—but Monica cannot tell about Josef. He likes to play cat and mouse.

Bless Gabrielle, who takes advantage of the lapse in conversation.

"Guess what, Papa? I'm learning to ride. Rosemary's got a new horse."

"Isn't that nice? What kind of a horse is it?" Josef appears to be fascinated.

"A quarterhorse, and Rosemary says if you want to ride her, she will let you, but not for more than an hour. We could go there after breakfast."

Monica hides a smile behind her napkin and David winks at her at the prospect of Josef's getting on a horse.

"Well, Gabrielle, I'm not sure I'll have time," he says judiciously, "although I would love to see Rosemary's horse. Tell me, what else do you do on this island? Do you like it here?"

"Of course I like it," she says, ruining everything. "I take piano lessons and I do ballet and we had a sports meet and guess what, Daddy? I'm Ms. Broad Jump of Genessee Island!"

"Ms. Broad Jump! Think of that! I never dreamed a daughter of mine would manage that. You and your mother are certainly big wheels around here."

"Josef, have some of these little cheese rolls. Remember, I used to make them for you? They were your favorites. And here's some raspberry jam to go with them . . ."

Monica jumps up to offer fruit to everyone. The atmosphere is becoming taut, as though invisible strings were stretched tightly everywhere. Somehow, nothing is working out, and Monica cannot really understand why. Suddenly Josef snaps his fingers. Does he have the answer?

"I forgot the champagne. How could I have been so careless!"

"Champagne? You want champagne now?" Irina asks. This is unexpected, but she wants to please Josef. "I think we have some wine; will that do?"

"Mother, I'm afraid the wine is all gone," Monica says quietly.

"Ah, but I have one bottle hidden away for special occasions. Of course, this is a special occasion. It's a good California Chardonnay!"

She rises to get it, but Josef protests. "It's all right, Irina. We don't have to have it. It's just that it goes with a certain announcement I want to make."

"But I'd love to! What better occasion?" Irina smiles gloriously as she leaves the room; she returns presently with the tall slender bottle. Monica sets out wineglasses and Irina fills them. Then Josef stands up, holds his glass high, and lets his eyes rest on the Bird, who blushes up at him and then bows her head and stares at her plate.

"You asked about the summer, Irina, and I told you about the trio. But I left out the main event. Melanie and I are getting married on the first of June. Come, dear, stand up and be seen!"

Monica claps her hand over her mouth to keep from shouting. Melanie springs up and settles back again, obviously embarrassed. She bends her long neck, the goose neck, over her plate, and Monica sees herself as the executioner who would gladly chop off her head.

Irina becomes chalk white; her hand shakes and the wine spills on the tablecloth. She opens her mouth as if to say something, but the words will not come. She places the wineglass on the table and a dreadful silence follows the toast. Gabrielle looks around the table and it is clear that she is puzzled. Then she breaks the stillness with her high voice.

"But Daddy, we thought you were going to marry Mama again."

"You thought *that*, Irina? You actually thought that I'd forget that you took the girls and ran off, ran away from me? Did you think there was a chance I'd come back to you after that? Oh, Irina!"

Josef sits down, laughs ironically, and sips the wine. Again the room falls into a tense silence. What is there to say now? What can anyone say? And then the silence is broken as the front doorbell rings—a weak, unpleasant ring, a metallic gargle.

"I'll go," Monica cries, getting up. Her face is flushed and a strand of dark hair sticks to her forehead. She does not know what to do, what to think, what to say, but at least answering the door is an escape. The door sticks and she must kick it before she can open it wide. At last it comes. And there, standing before her, dressed in her schoolgirl uniform topped with one of Irina's wilder sweaters, is the last person Monica wants to see. Sheila!

"Hello, Monica!" she says brightly.

Monica holds her forehead with her hand and is afraid she may faint. For a second she closes her eyes and groans; then she comes to her senses and lets Sheila walk in.

____3

The Question Is Answered

Sheila stands in the middle of the living room and even when nobody greets her, she smiles idiotically at the company seated around the table. "Well, hello, everybody," she says cheerfully. "Wow, you're the whole trio, aren't you? Hey, you were *good* last night. Really good. Super. Mr. Kroll, I never heard anyone play the violin like you. Wow! And when you and Mrs. Kroll danced together, you were so beautiful, I just couldn't believe it!"

The silence thickens, but she goes on.

"What I mean is that I just couldn't imagine my mother and father dancing like that. Or dancing at all. It must make you feel so marvelous to twirl around like that."

Josef growls a low impatient thank you.

"And Mrs. Kroll, I wanted you to know I bought one of your sweaters and I love it. I've never seen anything like this before."

"Thank you," Irina manages to say, but she does not invite Sheila to join them.

She has chosen the ugliest sweater of the lot, the craziest, most impossible of all, and it becomes even more ridiculous over her school uniform. Slowly Sheila realizes that nobody has said hello to her or invited her to sit down. Suddenly she knows she is out of place. She droops. Amazingly, Monica's aggravation with her roommate vanishes and she sees Sheila as unloved, defenseless, forever bumbling into the wrong place. Now she puts her arm around Sheila and introduces her.

"This is my roommate, Sheila Dawes," Monica says. Quietly and with dignity, she names each person around the table. That done, she leads Sheila quietly to the door and out to the porch.

"Sheila, I'd love to ask you in. Honest, I would. But you can see for yourself that things are awfully tense in there. A family matter. Look, I know I invited you down once, and I haven't forgotten."

Sheila appears hurt in spite of the apology.

"You do like Kathryn, don't you? She's glad to have you, I know." This may not be exactly the truth, but Monica lets it sink in. "Please, Sheila, try to understand. My father will go this afternoon and tonight I'm going out, but tomorrow morning please come over for breakfast and then we'll take a long walk together. See, I've really been thinking about you, and I've got something very important to tell you, something about yourself . . ."

"About me?" Sheila interrupts, and hope lights her eyes. Monica will have to think up something before the next day, and she will somehow—later. "It's okay, Monica. I guess I understand. I hope things work out for you, whatever it is. See you tomorrow."

She is still disappointed, but it is not the first time

she has been brushed off. As she walks down the path, something about her—perhaps the way one narrow shoulder is higher than the other, or something about the hair that hangs so lifelessly over the crazy sweater —touches Monica, and she thinks now that she must really help her and promises herself that she will.

When she returns to the dining room, Melanie Burd is standing, neither angry nor upset, simply a cool Bird who has made up her mind to leave.

"Just a minute," Irina says at last in a cold whisper that is almost a hiss. "It is incredible, Josef, that you would think of marrying a child like this. And you, Miss Burd . . ." Monica shivers for the pianist as her mother's eyes gleam at her. "Don't you have any sense in your head? You should be a concert pianist, not an accompanist. Why do you throw yourself away on a man twice your age? Will you tell me that?"

David attempts to lighten the atmosphere with a joke. "Good pianists are hard to find, Irina. You have to marry them to keep them." The joke fails.

Irina keeps on attacking the Bird, who does not flinch in the least. "You are very young, Miss Burd. Do you know what kind of man this is?"

"Yes, I do."

"Oh no you don't!" Irina continues in an icy voice. "Not only will you give up your career for this egotist —all artists are egotists, and Josef is no exception—but in ten years he will be an old man. He is past his prime and you haven't begun to reach yours. You will spend the best part of your life taking care of him."

"Irina, shut up!" Josef hisses. Monica wants to run away, but is rooted to the spot. Her mother is tense with growing rage and her father has slammed down his wineglass so hard that his wine joins Irina's in spilling on the tablecloth.

"Consider this before it's too late. Try to get some sense in your head," Irina says to Melanie.

"For God's sake, don't listen to that harpy," Josef cries.

"I'm leaving, Mrs. Kroll. Thank you for your hospitality."

Monica realizes that this Bird is not angry, not upset, not even sarcastic as she thanks Irina. She has made up her mind to leave and that is that. She has also made up her mind to marry Josef, and nothing anyone can say will deter her. Josef begs Melanie to stay, but she leaves, and David, embarrassed now, as the party is beyond saving, clears his throat and gets up as well.

"Irina, Josef, Monica . . . this seems to be a family affair and no place for an innocent cellist. Irina, you are a remarkable and beautiful woman, one of a kind. I thank you for all this"—a gesture sweeps the table—"and for your kindness. I'll see you later, Josef. Monica . . ."

David's sweetness shames them all and the battle stops momentarily. Gabrielle has fled but nobody has noticed. Monica stands near the door, cheeks flaming and eyes filled with defeat. It is all over now. The pain is so sharp and new that she cannot quite face it. David passes his hand over her hair, then leaves, understanding that she is hurt.

Once he has gone, however, the quarrel breaks loose like a storm, and it is Monica who turns on her father with the first lash.

"How could you do that, Dad, how could you be so mean and so thoughtless? How could you be so *cruel*, to bring that Burd person here, that cold fish! And make that dumb announcement! Mother only wanted the four of us to be together for a few hours, one Sunday morning. That's little enough to ask. Why did you have to spoil it?"

Josef draws himself up in anger. Monica has always been the good child, the obedient daughter, the loving princess.

"I am your father. This is no way to talk to me," he storms.

"What kind of father are you?" she says in a low tense voice that cuts through the room. Then she repeats it, shouting it so that it can be heard vibrating through the garden and up the road. "WHAT KIND OF FATHER ARE YOU?"

Irina jumps up and tries to quiet her, puts her arm around her, but Monica will not be stilled. All the hopes and love and forgiveness she has sustained for her father these last three years cannot put down the anger that rises in her now.

"You don't care about us, not one bit. You want me to stay the little girl who will sit on your lap because you're too vain to want a grown-up daughter around. You say what a pity it is that I don't play the piano anymore, but where were you when we first came here, when I called you and begged you to take me home? You knew that it was my dream to play, to accompany you. But there was not one word from you. Not one.

"Do you know who cares about us, who really cares? It's Mother. She's the one who insisted that I go to a good school. What do you care about us? You don't even send us half the money you're supposed to, and you never bothered to ask how Irina was getting along and if we had enough to eat and a place to live. And there are times when we *don't* have enough to eat. And look at you. You're getting fat, do you know that, you're getting *fat!*"

Irina tries to quiet her and to still Josef, whose eyes are blazing.

"Now listen to me, young lady, it was your mother who left me; it was your mother who ran off. You ought to know what a pepperpot she is; apparently you're just like her."

"If I am, I didn't know it until this minute. Of course Mother is quick-tempered; that's how she is because she's full of life. Did you think she could stand by and see you have affairs with one woman after another, and always someone young and innocent? Let me tell you this, Mother has always been faithful to you, and it's not for lack of opportunity, either. But you, you're full of vanity . . ."

"Now, now," Irina pleads in one last attempt to pull everything together. "Everyone's getting excited and angry. Let's be civil!"

"It's too late to be civil," Monica cries. "I *am* angry. Do you hear that, Daddy? You've treated Mother miserably, unkindly, cruelly. Aren't you a human being? Are you incapable of feeling for anyone but yourself?"

"That's enough, Monica," Irina begs. "Please stop now. You've said enough."

But Monica cannot stop. "Don't you know what it's like to try to make ends meet, to have to pay the rent with nothing to support you but a little job here, a little ballet teaching there? She cuts the hair of the man who owns the fish market just to keep us in food. In fish heads. Did you know that? Did you?"

She stops to catch her breath. Josef stares at her, dumbfounded. She speaks more calmly now. "You can't be a very smart man, Daddy, not very smart at all, because what you don't know is that Irina is a wonderful woman and one of a kind and you will never find anyone like her anywhere. You will make an idiot of yourself over that cold Burd turd, whatever she is, but she will never in all her life be able to give you one ounce of joy. It's not in her."

"Enough!" Josef lashes out, and Monica flinches, fearing he will strike her. "In Europe you would be whipped for this outrageous behavior."

"This isn't Europe," Monica retorts.

"You leave her alone, Josef," Irina cries, standing in front of Monica to protect her. "She's right!"

"She's getting to be a harpy like you!"

Smash! A plate flies across the room, hits the wall, and breaks into a hundred pieces. Irina and Josef stand facing each other. These two who danced in such harmony not twelve hours before are barking insults at each other in English, Italian, Hungarian. Are these her parents, then, this thin blazing-eyed woman who holds still another plate in her hand, ready to throw, and this smallish round man with the growing bald spot—an angry man who has nearly struck his daughter and may possibly strike his former wife? Is this what she has dreamed about for so long? Anger turns to anguish.

"Stop, both of you, please stop! Mother, you've already smashed one of your good plates, and that's the only other one we have. Dad, please, both of you, let's be civil! Please, just this once let's be peaceful!"

For a moment they stop to stare at her. Since when does Monica consider herself an adult, on their level?

At that very moment the doorbell rings its harsh unpleasant voice. Irina puts the plate back on the table and Josef rearranges his facial expression, but Monica buries her face in her hands as David Rosling walks in.

"Sorry to interrupt you all," he says pleasantly, if somewhat sheepishly, "but I wonder, did I leave my cigarettes here?"

Irina and Monica search for them everywhere while Josef stands at the window and frowns at a sparrow sitting outside on a sprig of lilac.

"I can't find them anywhere," Irina says. "Are you sure you left them here?"

"I thought so. It doesn't really matter. Would there be a place here where I could get some?" he asks, a boyish innocence blooming about him.

"Yes, there is. The drugstore," Irina answers curtly, meaning she wants to be left alone.

"Monica, go with him. Show him where the drugstore is," Josef orders. But Monica remains where she is out of stubbornness. She doesn't have to obey her father anymore. It is Irina who appeals to her daughter in a quivering voice.

"Darling, please go," she says.

Monica looks from one parent to the other. Perhaps they will fight or perhaps they will talk calmly now. Is it possible they will make up? It is the old pattern appearing again, love and hate and love and hate. Fight and make up. It can happen too often.

"All right," she says, two words that indicate she has accepted defeat. She walks into the useless sunshine of the late morning and David follows.

4

David and Monica

She is determined not to cry, but does not trust herself to speak. She wants only to leave, to get away from home, from this island, as fast as possible. Immediately. If she had wings, she would rise and take off. No wings, no magic carpet, so she must nod hello politely to the people who pass her on their way to church, or home from church—she could not care less.

"This way," she says to David, leading him to the store that stays open on Sunday. David walks beside her and says nothing. When they get to the store, she says, "Here it is!" Her voice is so mournful that David puts a sympathetic hand on her shoulder and does not try to smile or make jokes.

"I have a confession to make," he says. "I gave up smoking two years ago and I'm not ready to begin again."

"Very funny," she says in a choked voice. So agitated that she cannot stand there, she walks down to the shore. David walks with her to the end of the wharf and gazes across the smooth water that mirrors the sky. A gull swims unconcerned, waiting for a fish.

"It was an awkward way of getting you out of there," David apologizes, "and a terribly feeble excuse. But I think they wanted to be alone."

"Because they are such lovers, I suppose," she says sarcastically. "They are impossible people, absolutely impossible, my father especially. I know that my mother appears giddy, like a child, in a way, but my father should know that, should be able to see beyond that. If only you knew how my mother worked for this morning's reunion! My father is so gross!"

"Come now, Monica, they are simply very human."

"Is tearing each other apart *human*?" she asks.

"Possibly. Monica, why don't we go somewhere that's not quite so public?" he suggests. Is she shouting? Being crude? Talking too loud? She can't blame him for not wanting to walk beside such an emotionally unbalanced person. She fears that she is close to sobbing; the tears sting her eyes even as she begs them to hold off. She walks rapidly from the wharf to a small winding path where there are no other people, a path that runs along the shore. David walks beside her.

"Monica, I'd like to ask you a favor."

"More cigarettes?" She did not mean to sound so harsh and resentful; it was only a way of holding back the tears. Please let him understand!

"No, of course not, Monica. That really was clumsy of me; I can be such a goof. I was just wondering if we could go for a boat ride or rent a rowboat here."

"I can borrow one. Do you know how to row?" she asks. Somehow he seems such a city person that she cannot quite see him rowing. No matter, she can manage.

"I've seen it in the movies." He grins. At any other time she would grin back, but her sense of humor has abandoned her for the moment. Everything has blown up; it is a catastrophe so great she cannot begin to contemplate it. It is a relief to find a boat for David— something to do. She leads him along a narrow path to a quiet cove where Dennis and Tom keep a rowboat; they will not mind if she uses it. The sun slants through the new green of the birch trees and lights up the unfolding ferns. David stops to touch them.

"Fantastic! They're real. Actually growing and not made of plastic. What form! Beautiful, aren't they?"

Monica nods. "We eat the fern fronds. Like the Indians."

"How exotic! Are they good?"

"Yes, very good. And it's not exotic of us. Sometimes our funds get low. One of the things my mother loves about the Island is that you can gather clams, fish, and eat fern fronds and dandelion greens."

"That's enchanting."

"Not when you have to do it," Monica replies. They pass an abandoned picnic table in a grove of birches and David confesses that he is tired; could they sit here for just a few minutes? Monica suspects he is not the least bit weary but sits beside him on the table, their feet planted on the bench. Now David becomes serious.

"Irina and Josef have to live their own lives," he says, there being no point in going on about ferns and woodlands. "And you have to live yours. It's unfortunate that we can't make other people live the way we think they should, but that's how it is."

Monica will not discuss her parents anymore: family problems should be kept at home. She sighs a long shuddering sigh and then tears fall in torrents and she sobs. She hates crying like this, particularly in front of someone else, and most particularly in front of David, with whom she danced so happily the night before, yet she cannot seem to stop. David knows exactly what to do, does not beg her to stop, does not offer consolations or put his arm around her. When he sees that she has her own handkerchief, he does not offer his, but waits until the spasm of crying is over, finished with a firm wipe of her eyes and a stern nose-blowing. She knows she must look red-eyed, moist-nosed, and hideous, but it's beyond repair now.

"My parents, Josef and Irina, can both . . . go . . . jump in the lake."

"That might be awfully good for them, I suppose," David agrees.

"They are nothing but children. They have to be applauded all the time, both of them. My father *must* be adored or he wilts. For my mother, everything is show and tell. But I'm tired of applauding. I just want them to be my parents and myself their daughter."

"Yes, but you're sort of a big daughter, aren't you? Kind of big to be wanting to climb back into the nest?"

"That's a mean thing to say," she flashes at him, but she realizes that she has not seen it in just that way before. He has cut to the heart of the matter.

"Isn't that really why you want to go back to California? To be the little girl in the nice suburban nest, like a million other little girls?"

"That's only part of it. Mostly, I guess I've been cut off from my father and I wanted to be with him, even though I'd be there for just my last year of school. I thought I could keep house for him. I suppose the Bird will do that now. Anyway, is it so out of line to want to live in what you call 'a nice suburban nest'?"

"It's not wrong, but I don't think it would work. Remember that phrase, 'You can't go home again'? You've gone way beyond La Californie. You might even find it stifling."

"Not for a minute. But if it wouldn't work for me, what about my mother? What is to become of her?

She's having a hard time, David. And incredible as it may sound, she really thinks my father is the only man in the world for her. How can he even dream of marrying that cold fish? And to tell my mother about it in such a cruel way! Melanie Burd. The Melancholy Bird!"

"Josef can be anything but tactful," David admits, "and possibly he wanted to make your mother suffer a little. I don't really know." He begins to smile. "The Melancholy Bird! A good name for her. Sometimes she seems exactly like that, but it's only a first impression. Too bad you don't know her, Monica. She's not what she seems."

"I don't want to know her. Disgusting, dull turd-bird."

"I gather you don't like her. Did you think she played well last night?"

"Oh yes, no doubt about that. She was first-rate. But that's no reason for my father to marry her."

"Then you think they should continue to live together without being married? Actually, Melanie is a fine pianist, and your mother is right when she says she will give up her 'big career' if she marries Josef. Melanie knows all that. She wraps her life around two things—music and your father. In a way, she complements your father. He needs her calmness. She needs his vivacity. Your parents are really too much the same."

"Paprika and hot pepper. Hot and cold. Sweet and sour. That's true, but they *understand* each other. And my father has responsibilities, has had them, but refuses to recognize them. If I'm going to the Chatham School, it's thanks to my mother, who made me, but look at Gabrielle. She is bright and a talented dancer but doesn't even know it. She'll go to waste on this island, for one thing, and she really needs a father, for another. I don't want her to be wasted the way I was."

"Wasted? What do you mean?"

"I don't know what my father has told you, but he always insisted that I study piano with the very best teachers; I worked very hard. Mostly I wanted to become his accompanist. But when we came here, when my mother forced us to come here, he simply forgot about us. It was the end of music for me."

"The end of music? Didn't you shout about it, complain bitterly, demand lessons?"

"Of course I complained. I even ran away once, but my father wouldn't take responsibility for me. I wrote to him about it, many letters. Never an answer. He didn't care."

"Maybe you had the wrong address. Or someone else got your letters."

"I used to make up excuses like that, David. But the address was right; and I dropped the letters in the mailbox myself. I never could see it as clearly as I do now. He didn't care, David, and that's the truth."

"Hold on! I think he cared very much and thought about it a great deal. Don't be too hard on him. He may have thought it was best for you to turn elsewhere. The world is full of girls who are promising young pianists, like you, but very few get anywhere with it. It's a difficult life, and he may well have been trying to protect you."

"But he never said that. He wrote only once, a short note of congratulation when I received a scholarship at Chatham."

"Let's look at it this way. If you meant to become a pianist, it was your responsibility to do something about it, no matter how careless Irina was or how indifferent your father seemed. That's not easy to take, is it? Monica, let me tell you something about Melanie. Her parents had plenty of money but didn't want her to be a musician, so she walked out on them without a cent—literally. She practically starved while living in Berkeley and didn't want anyone to know it. And she became a pianist, a good one. Does that say anything to you?"

Monica becomes warm and her face reddens. She wants to cry out and walk away. Yet she says nothing and she stays. For the first time she sees that if she were a genuine musician, she would have fought, scratched, begged, run away, or done anything to stay with her music. She can no longer blame her father or her mother, but only herself.

"I'm not really a musician, then, I guess," she says at last, quietly. And with that, a certain knot of hard resentment that has been within her for so long now loosens. She breathes a deep trembling breath and feels lighter now, calmer. She slips her hand into David's, and they jump down from the table and walk together along the path.

"It no longer seems such a tragedy—my piano, that is," she says.

"That's good. It's not a tragedy at all. There are other things."

"But I had a chance. And Gabrielle should have her chance too. Good teachers, good instruction, at least a sense of what ballet is all about."

"I know what you're saying," David agrees, and then he cries excitedly, "Look at those geese over there! What a lot of them! Aren't they marvelous?"

"They're ducks, not geese, but that's all right," Monica says of the flock that are flying over the water, their wings beating hard. "Geese come to the Island too. Sometimes I've seen as many as sixty standing near the lake. There *is* a lake here, you know. I can never get over their beauty; they're very bright, too."

"I'd love to see them. This is *some* place! Perhaps I'll come up here for a few days this summer, if I can get away."

"Really? You could stay with us," she says politely, and her heart jumps. She would like it very much if he were to come. The thought of it hides the deeper pain of the morning.

When they pull out the rowboat, David asks if he may row, for he would love to try it. He splashes around the quiet cove in circles until Monica has a hard time not laughing, for she has never seen anyone so awkward. She corrects his grip and explains the simple principles, and he improves so rapidly that she realizes he has known how to manage a boat all along and only wanted to make her laugh. Eventually he rows smoothly along the shore and Monica lets her fingers trail in the cool water. She cannot assess the depth of her wound, and she decides she must be careful not to cry about it anymore, at least not in front of David. She speaks of it only once.

"Isn't it strange, David? The Bird—I mean, Melanie —will be taking my mother's place as his wife and my place as his daughter, 'the accompanist.' "

"Not at all. Those are only terms, Monica. Nobody in all this world can take Irina's place. If I were Josef, I could never let her go, believe me. She's superb and unique—and you are too, pet. You can't be replaced by anyone. It's time for someone to find out exactly how special you are. See?"

It is the choicest compliment she has ever had, and

will be especially treasured because David is honest with her even when it means giving her pain. For a second she thinks of Courtney; he would be incapable of such directness and understanding.

David has begun to hum; then he interrupts himself to remark about the water.

"I've never seen it so clear. Just look, Monica. You can see every stone, every pebble. Are those minnows, those tiny fish? And the sun reflections. Do you think, as I do, that this is all remarkable?"

"Yes." But it is David, she thinks, who is even more remarkable. Nobody has ever made her see the truth of her own life so directly.

They row quietly and David hums a melody— Mozart?—and Monica thinks how good it is to let the sun shine on her face while David manages the oars with easy rhythmic strokes and she can let the pain wait until she must face it—later.

Too soon it is time to go back. They tie the boat as they found it and walk along the path, hand in hand. When they finally stand in front of Bittersweet Place, he hesitates.

"When will I see you again?"

"I don't know. It's not likely that I'll be going to California."

"There are other places."

"Could be."

"Monica, I might make it to the Island again, or there's Vancouver. It's really not at all far from Berkeley. Could I see you there, call for you at your school?"

She smiles up at him, says of course, but does not dare to hope that anything will come of this vague promise.

"I'll send you postcards from my gypsy travels."

"I'd love to hear from you, David."

He bends down to kiss her good-bye, a kind and gentle kiss. If he comes back, she thinks, perhaps he will be her lover. It is a very consoling, even exciting thought, but she is finished with dreaming.

5

Aftermath

The house is silent, but Monica senses the echoes of a fight, of words hurled like daggers across a room, and it seems that the very air itself has been churned up and has not yet settled.

Is it possible her father has left without saying good-bye? Nowhere is there a note, a message, or a sign.

Nor, apparently, has Gabrielle returned, but Louka is very much there on the table. Who let her out of the laundry room? Nobody. It is cat magic. Monica, no longer gentle, pulls her angrily from the table where she has been polishing off the last of the caviar.

"Bad cat!"

But it is useless to punish her. She is simply a cat, acting in cat ways, just as her mother is Irina and so acts in that way—and Monica supposes she too acts in her fashion, whatever that may be. Still, she puts Louka out and locks the door.

The table, so recently a masterpiece, is now a ruin, the remains of a scene of battle. Portions of cheese, meat, half-eaten buns, and dabs of jam remain on the plates. A knife full of cream cheese rests on the delicate cloth, spreading a thin film of grease. Someone has spilled the plum jam. Wine stains the tablecloth where her parents spilled it. Half a cup of once vibrant and expensive Colombian coffee sits abandoned. Crumpled napkins, a stray sardine, a fallen glass. Louka, she thinks, has dragged two cheese buns over the floor.

Monica cannot bear to remain there and hurries upstairs, where she hears the sound of muffled weeping and finds her mother curled up under the covers in her room, a box of Kleenex beside her. Monica is nearly moved to tears once more by the convulsive rising and falling of Irina's shoulders, and she longs to escape the despair that permeates the house. Yet she sits on the edge of the bed. Presently her mother's long sensitive hand reaches out to her and she holds it.

"He's left, then, has he?"

Her mother nods but says nothing.

"It's not really such a tragedy," Monica says. "He behaved so badly."

"It's his nature," Irina says. "I should have known better."

"It was his fault, not yours. Mother, let's get off this island, go somewhere else where we've never been before, and start over. What do you think?"

"Later, Monica. I can't think now. My head aches. I think I need to sleep."

"Sure, Mother," Monica says. "I'll clean up downstairs. Don't worry about it. Do you want a cup of tea?"

"Later, not now."

Monica covers her mother with a wool coverlet. For all that the sun shines, the house is chilly. Downstairs she finds a green felt pen and writes on two pieces of cardboard DO NOT DISTURB. She tacks one on the front door and one on the back door. Today her mother will want to be alone.

The house takes on an unnatural quiet. It was like this when her grandmother died and nobody dared to talk except in low whispers. Only the sound of low quiet weeping and an occasional street noise interrupted the strange quiet then.

"But nobody has died here," Monica reasons, "only an idea. An illusion. A silly dream."

Nevertheless, such a defeat is not easy to take. She wants to flee, to leave this oppressive atmosphere as soon as she can. Quickly she clears the table, wrapping the food carefully and placing it in the refrigerator. Everything must be saved. She covers the cheeses so they will not dry out, wraps every bit of meat, places the cherished butter in a bowl with a lid, and puts the buns and pastries in plastic bags. She even pours the coffee into a bottle, for much as they disdain heated-over coffee, this will have to do. The demolished feast will have to last them a long time.

The table is cleared, the dishes scraped and soaking, and the precious tablecloth placed in a laundry tub full of water so that the stains will disappear. How exhausted she is! One would think she hadn't slept for a month.

One last trip upstairs to change to her jeans, wash her face, and brush her hair listlessly. From the window she can see Jim Weed walking up to the door, but he must have seen the sign, for he turns and wanders off again. Later he will be a comfort to Irina.

And now she must be alone, must somehow get away. She throws a poncho over her shoulders and leaves the house.

_____6

Monica Alone

When you are on an island there is no place to run except in circles or possibly up, up as high above everything else as you can possibly get. And that is where Monica is going now, hurrying along the blue macadam road, hoping she will not meet anyone she knows—up to the crest of Mount Albert, which is the one place on this island she regards as sacred.

Of course there is _The Genessee Queen_, which could take her away entirely, but she is not ready yet for that trip. There is still so much to take care of here on the Island.

The climb up Mount Albert is a long, difficult three-mile ascension, making every muscle ache. So much the better! She walks fast. Perspiration stains her shirt before she has gone very far, and she must tie her red kerchief around her head to keep her forehead dry.

What comfort David was able to give checked the pain when it was too new to be faced directly. Now she has no choice but to probe it.

She passes a patch of woods where Crazy Hattie lives in a hut that is twisted askew like a witch's hovel in a fairy tale. Poor Hattie, who loves Irina's mad skirts! What made her so embittered? Monica recalls a rumor about a husband who deceived her and ran off with someone else. Did she never get over her anger, then? Was she so unable to forget the wrong done her that she has devoted her whole life to it?

Monica stops short, for it now seems possible that this could happen to Irina. But it mustn't! Monica feels an unexpected wave of love and caring for her mother. Somehow she must be rescued, cared for, encouraged to "open her hand and let the bird fly away." But how?

She walks more slowly now, for her head begins to ache and this climb is long, difficult, and endless. It is a nightmare in which she will climb and climb and climb forever.

The nightmare fades as she enters the wooded park at the top of the mountain, breathes the fir-fragrant air, and passes through a cathedral of vast towering cedars, pines, and firs that reach up into the sky. The Indians believed that a spirit lived in each tree. If she were to sit here very still, could they make her wiser and more serene?

Fortunately, few cars are parked here, and the visitors who have come to take in the view seem to be leaving. They smile at her, but she avoids their glances. She wants only to be alone. The knots in her thighs and the calves of her legs ache and she is worn out with the heat, for she has climbed too quickly. But this will be easier to deal with than that other hurt that has become a physical ache inside her.

She crosses the crest of the mountain—easily

rounded rocks here—and sits on a ledge that overhangs the steep side of the mountain so that there seems to be nothing below her but a long depth of air. She pulls up her knees and rests her head on them, still breathing heavily from the climb, yet more and more easily now as she lets her eyes travel over what must be one of the most splendid landscapes she has ever seen. Evergreens fringe the plunging mountainside, and at the base she sees a grove of firs—it is as though she were looking down from an airplane. From that grove at the base of the mountain the land stretches out, sloping slightly, then becoming flat and open to the sky. Here is a collage of stripes, patches, and squares of farmland, yellow or newly green with fresh crops and sometimes a rich brown where the earth has just been plowed.

And there is the Tanaka farm, set apart from the others. Flowers grow in long even strips of color, and the small house seems to sit in an island of moss or jade, with a small patch of blue that is a pond. A small and orderly paradise on this island.

For some people, then, like the Tanakas and Kathryn and Jim Weed and possibly Courtney, the Island is a paradise. For others, like Irina, it is a stopping place, a land where one can be apart for a while yet must not stay.

The fields below give way to a beach of white sand that stretches out between two long spurs of rock enclosing a small bay, which opens into a vast wideness of water gleaming blue in the afternoon sun. The islands far out in the water take on the mounded shapes that could be whales or tortoises or sleeping girls. As they extend farther and farther back they become mistier; there are so many shades of blue she cannot count them. And above all this is the sky, a cool azure blue, a northern sky on a sun-filled afternoon.

"If I sit here long enough, straight-backed and still as a monk at meditation, will this view cure me?" she wonders. Will its vastness shrink the pain until it is no more substantial than a butterfly that has just appeared to flutter before her, fearless over the vast drop of space under it?

She remains motionless on the rock, without thinking, without feeling, without moving, until a distant whistle pricks her ears. *The Genessee Queen*! First she hears it, then she sees it as it rounds the bend of the Island, gleaming white and moving in dignity through the blue waters. The air is so clear she can even see the red maple leaf on the white silk of the Canadian flag that flies from its mast. A foaming path follows *The Genessee Queen*, and in a short while disappears.

And that's where her father must be, down there on that ferry, which, from this vantage point, seems no bigger than a toy. Her father, David, and Melanie Burd, all three. Does her father think of her, she wonders, as he sits on the deck flicking ashes from his cigar? Does he stand at the rail with Melanie, or does he stand alone, watching Genessee growing smaller and smaller behind him? She can almost hear him saying, "Well, so much for Irina and the girls!"

"We don't matter to him," she says out loud. "We happened to him long ago and when we left him, that was good-bye. The rest was all illusion. Now we *know* it's finished."

"Good-bye! Good-bye! Good-bye!" she says out loud three times—the magic number. A tiny voice on a mountaintop. Soon the ferry will disappear beyond that last mound of rock and she will never see her father again as far as she knows; and if she does, they will be strangers to each other.

The ferry appears once more in the far distance, looking more than ever like a toy on the water. She imagines a string that leads from her hand to this proud boat. If she wishes, she can wind up the string and pull the ferry back to shore and keep her father with her forever. But it's too late. She cannot do this, not even in her imagination. She lets the string out, then opens her hand and lets it fall. The ferry with her father on it may sail where it will.

With that she lets out a long pent-up sigh, then curls up on the ledge and immediately falls asleep.

It is a deep, intense sleep, and whether it has lasted ten minutes or an hour and ten, she cannot tell, but the voices of visiting sightseers wake her. Sitting up with a start, aware that she is noticed, she hides her head in her arms, ashamed at having been caught in such a personal act as a nap. She remains motionless in this curled-up position until the visitors leave.

It is curious that she feels so rested, so utterly calm. The problems that have been muddying her mind these last days—or these last years—have now settled, and she is as clear as the water she and David peered into that very morning.

When she returns to school, she will take down that too-young, too-romantic photograph of her father and place it somewhere else, at the bottom of her sweater drawer or inside a scrapbook (should she ever get a scrapbook). If she feels anything now, it is a promise of peace, the sense of completion, of a question answered, of a theme of music resolved at last, as in the Franck sonata.

What now? She must help Irina. Irina who has been so good, puzzling Irina who can be so difficult, Irina who needs her now. But good heavens, what *can* she do? She will think of something.

And Sheila . . . she had almost forgotten about Sheila.

And Courtney! Now she jumps up. She promised to go there for dinner and here it is late afternoon. They'll be expecting her. Courtney and his father can't wait to show her the boat. Within seconds she is running, leaping, flying down the mountain road toward home.

————7

Dinner at Courtney's

Irina has left a note.

Monica, I've gone to the store to straighten it out. Gabrielle's staying at Rosemary's. See you later, darling.

Monica bathes, dresses in the long denim skirt, which will be formal enough to please Mrs. Phillips, and examines herself in the mirror to see if the emotions of the day have ravaged her face. There she appears a trifle reserved, perhaps: she practices smiling, for they will expect her to smile, and mimicks herself praising the boat, the roast beef, and the Yorkshire pudding. "I'll be okay," she promises herself; and she leaves a note for Irina, takes the bicycle, and pedals across the island to West Shore.

"Hello, hello! I knew you wouldn't forget!" Courtney says as he wipes his hands on a rag, puts it back on the unfinished boat, and walks over to Monica. He puts his arm around her and kisses her softly. "We've had a day of problems! Phew! Finished a board and no sooner did we get it on than it split. And something's not quite right with the mast, but . . . come on, we'll show you."

"Looks great to me," Monica says.

Mr. Phillips comes forward to greet her. "Maybe you can help us decide on the stain. Court likes it darker, I like it lighter. We've been waiting all day for a more considered opinion. Here are the samples."

Monica laughs lightly, as she is meant to do. "*My* opinion? What do I know about it? I like them both; they're so striking!"

They talk with her as though nothing has gone amiss, as if everything were exactly as it was yesterday or two months ago or even last year. Monica thinks of David briefly; he would have known instantly that something had happened and would have found an excuse to pull her aside and find out what, knowingly, comfortingly. Courtney and his father josh one another lightly as they talk and think of nothing but the boat, though at one point Courtney grins in his good-looking way and mentions that it was a great party the night before, and Mr. Phillips remembers to add that Mr. Kroll is a superb violinist.

"Thank you," she says demurely.

Mrs. Phillips comes to the door, rings a small silver

bell, and calls out in a soprano voice, "Yoo-hoo, time to come in now or that lovely roast will burn to pieces. And Monica, my dear, I'm so glad you could come!"

"It's nice of you to ask me," she says. "May I help you?"

"Oh no, no, no! Doris and I are managing very well. Come in and sit down."

While the men wash, Monica sits in the living room of this house she once admired so much; once she wanted one exactly like it. Everything here is the same as it was last year and the year before that. The portrait of Queen Elizabeth with a sash across her bosom and medals looks down from her place of honor over the fireplace. A moth-eaten deer's head stares from its place over a brown bookcase, and in the dining room the British flag, which is at least cheerfully colored, covers the wall over the oak sideboard. Even with the flag, one feels that everything here is unadulterated beige- or putty-colored and that it will never change.

Even Mrs. Phillips and the unhappy Doris are having a tiff in the kitchen, just as they did the last time Monica came to dinner.

"Doris, you may put butter *or* cream in the mashed potatoes, but *never* butter *and* cream! Good heavens, will you never learn?"

Doris mumbles, sniffs, and answers back in a surly rudeness calculated to exasperate her mother. Monica closes her ears, doesn't want to hear any more, and is relieved when Courtney comes back and they all sit down around the table.

"You look nice, dear," Mrs. Phillips says to Monica, as much to pique Doris as anything. Mr. Phillips remarks that the dinner looks very nice. The word "nice" is well exercised here. Everything is "nice." The roast beef and Yorkshire pudding (which Mrs. Phillips makes well—and should, after ever so many Sundays of practice, year after year), the overboiled Brussels sprouts, and the simple pudding for dessert with the promise of a trifle next time is exactly like all the dinners Monica has eaten here. During the dinner Mrs. Phillips brings up her dislike for socialism and the errors of the Immigration Policy and then wonders if the Island really should try to enlarge the Festivals because "so many strangers and odd types are beginning to come over."

Monica nods her head noncommittally when Mrs. Phillips asks her if she doesn't agree, and then Mr. Phillips clears his throat and asks Monica about school. It is a relief when tea is finished and everyone gets up.

"May I help with the dishes? I'd love to," Monica says, but this time Courtney objects, swinging her around to face him.

"No, Monica, no! We're going to take a little walk. I've been waiting all day. We've been here long enough."

"Oh, you," Mrs. Phillips says. "Where are you going?"

"Out, to walk off this marvelous dinner," Courtney says, and Monica cannot really tell if he is sarcastic or not.

"It was very good, particularly after Chatham cuisine!" Monica says. "Thanks very much for asking me."

"Our pleasure," Mr. Phillips says, "and by the way, give my regards to your mother. I hadn't realized what a fine dancer she is until last night. Fascinating."

"Now, Randolph," Mrs. Phillips says, wagging her forefinger to chide him. "But of course, Monica, he's right. Your mother dances very well."

"We'll be leaving early in the morning, but it's not long until summer and I expect we'll see you then, Monica." Mr. Phillips smiles.

"Of course," says Mrs. Phillips, "and now let's let these two go. I can see Courtney getting ready to explode. Go ahead, dears. See you later."

Courtney and Monica walk along the beach, pick up stones and scale the waves, jog for half a mile, and then climb out on some rocks that jut out of the water. The setting sun casts pink reflections on the gulf and lights up Courtney's profile, that nearly perfect profile with the aggressive nose.

He caresses her dark hair with its auburn aura. "Monica, you were a vision last night. And you are beautiful to me tonight. Like a mermaid sitting on the rocks."

She laughs lightly. "How poetic you are!"

"Not really. I think we ought to talk—about something besides boat varnish—don't you? Really talk. You must know that you mean a lot to me."

"That's good. It means a lot to me to know you too, Courtney."

"I want to see more of you. Up until now it's been more or less an Island friendship, you might say. I want something more than that. I think we're ready for it."

"What do you have in mind?" she asks, glancing at him sideways, waiting as he grins, peers down at his Adidas as if he could find the answer there, and then faces her directly.

"It's awfully early to say. Mostly, something more than we have now. For one thing, I'd like to see you in Vancouver now and then; I'd like to invite you to the games and some of the things that go on at the University, and, if you liked, I wouldn't mind seeing you at Elizabeth Chatham. Maybe we could go out to dinner, the theater, dancing, something like that."

"That would be very nice," she says, for strangely enough she hadn't thought about a possible last year at Chatham, having hoped so intensely that she would be at Berkeley. She smiles pleasantly at Courtney. The girls of the Midnight Club would approve, be impressed, and she would get out once in a while.

"But there's something more too, Monica. I guess it happened last night when I saw you dancing with that tall fellow, that cellist, what's-his-name. It made me furious. I never expected it, but it did."

"I can't imagine why," she says, although she knows exactly what he means. "You and I danced together, Courtney."

"I know, and it was wonderful. But I don't want to share you with anyone. I guess that's it. I want you to dance with me, and have dinners with me, and go out with me—wait until the boat is finished—and go sailing with me. And nobody else."

"But Courtney, that's asking a lot. I couldn't dream of asking you not to see any other girl."

"That's different."

"Different for you than for me?"

"Sure it is. What I'm saying, Monica, is that I'm serious about you. Lots of times I dream of the two of us living here on the Island. Maybe we could build a house of our own, be perfectly content to stay here, never go anywhere else."

"You mean you'd be content not to go anywhere else at all? Aren't you even curious?"

He looks out toward Japan. "I'd be curious to see how far the boat would go. We might even make it from here to Hawaii. Or farther."

It's not at all what she had in mind.

"Of course I've got to finish college, go to graduate school, maybe get launched in Vancouver. But it would be a shame to waste all that time before we got married. Maybe when you're through Chatham, we can find an apartment in Vancouver. I think that even this coming summer should find us closer together. You know what I mean."

With this he pulls her toward him and kisses her long and hard. His hands caress her, but before he becomes too intimate she pulls away. Unthrilled. It's not at all what she expected, somehow, although she once dreamed of Courtney's making love to her.

"You really care about me seriously, then?" she asks.

"Yes. Just the two of us together from now on, forever. Maybe that's a little old-fashioned . . ."

"An apartment in Vancouver isn't exactly old-fashioned, or having an affair here, which I guess is what you mean, isn't it?"

"If only you knew how much I want you . . ."

She looks into the cool blue eyes, takes in the good-looking features, and understands at last the jutting nose. He wants her, of course, to be his exclusively, to be owned by him as he owns his dog and his boat. It almost appears arranged; she will become part of the family. There will be roast beef and overboiled Brussels sprouts every Sunday for the rest of her life, games and football matches in Vancouver while they are there, and life laid out in predictable patterns.

"Courtney," she says very gently, "do you know you've never really asked me anything? About my family, where we've been, what's happened to us, what I'm really like, what I really think?"

"Well, I imagine we'd come to that sooner or later, all that introspective stuff. I've been honest with you. You know what I want."

"Sure, Courtney." It's true, he has told her about his courses, the graduate work he will take, the firms he hopes to work with, the way he will vote, and his preference in shirts.

Suddenly she longs for David and knows that nothing will work with Courtney, nothing beyond a certain friendship. She touches his cheek with her hand.

"Courtney, thanks for everything. Let's be friends, shall we? But I can't own anyone, can't bear to be owned either. At least not for a long time. I'd like to see you whenever you feel like it, to go walking or swimming or have a good long talk, if you like."

"That's not exactly what I had in mind," he says, downcast now, his pride hurt. He is used to immediate success.

"There!" she says, kissing him quickly. "I'll see you again soon. But now I've got to get home."

"But it's vacation for you," he cries, sulking.

"Not really." She smiles, thinking of Irina and of Gabrielle and of Humpty-Dumpty as well. Everything must be put back together again. And Courtney does not suspect that anything has happened.

They stand up and walk slowly toward the house, where she has left her bicycle. She has received her first proposal on this day and turned it down—all in a way of speaking, of course. Courtney kisses her good night, but she knows he is puzzled by her reluctance, and therefore he is cooler and already more distant than before.

"I'll see you," he says as she gets on her bicycle.

"Of course. And good night, Courtney."

She bicycles home alone but does not mind.

EPILOGUE

————1

Sheila

Thoroughly exhausted, Monica sleeps without dreaming, as if all dreams had vanished, and she is grateful to drop out of the world for a few hours. It is not a dream but Kathryn's voice, a real voice, that calls up the stairs and awakens her.

"Hallo, hallooo! Is anybody around?"

Monday morning! Sheila! She had forgotten.

"Hi! I'm here. I'll be right down," Monica calls.

Apparently Irina has overslept too, for there she is in the hall, blowing kisses and apologies to Kathryn as she slips into a bathrobe and walks downstairs, less energetically than usual, Monica thinks while she herself rushes to get into jeans and a sweater. Gabrielle's voice can be heard chirping below as she comes in the back door.

Sheila, grinning, presents Monica with a loaf of somewhat heavy brown bread. "We both made it, Kathryn and I. And it has six different grains in it. Fantastic! I never made bread before."

"Isn't that wonderful!" Monica says, and Irina manages to beam at Sheila, who seems to have picked up some of Kathryn's spirit, for her eyes are shining and she seems to have lost some of the whining quality in her voice. She picks up Louka and babbles to Monica about having tried to throw a pot on Kathryn's wheel and what a mess it was, but oh she loves the Island and she is going to come back here . . .

As Irina puts the coffee on the stove, her eyebrows knit, and she queries Monica silently, asking if there is something wrong with this girl—is she drunk or crazy? Monica whispers to her mother not to worry, she gets like this when she is happy, which is only five percent of the time, but at the same time Monica suspects that in a subtle way Sheila has changed.

It is too treacherous to risk returning to the dining room for breakfast after Sunday's disaster there, so the five of them sit around the kitchen table, which is not only more intimate, but is bathed in the blessing of a direct ray of sunlight.

How wise Kathryn is, how wise and how good a friend, knowing exactly when to come! She must surely have guessed that Irina's plans have failed and that Irina, being the way she is, which is either very high or very low, is most likely numbed by what has happened. So Kathryn talks in her calm voice to keep up a certain easy momentum of conversation, as though everything is all right this sunny Monday morning. Irina takes out her long ivory holder and smokes, blowing curls of smoke through the ray of sunlight; now and then she smiles politely or answers a simple question. Monica is relieved that her mother is somewhat restored, but she aches for the sadness she senses in every word, every movement of the long delicate hand. Gabrielle insists on sitting in her mother's lap, which is a kind of comfort, and Monica is grateful to her for that.

But Sheila is making signs to Monica, and then she

remembers she promised to tell Sheila something important. Good heavens, what will it be? They will take a long walk and perhaps she will think of it.

"Mother, I promised Sheila we'd go out clamming today. So I think we'd better start."

"Yes, because I have to take the ferry this afternoon after lunch," Sheila adds. "And I thank you so much, Mrs. Kroll. Monica tells me the most wonderful things about you all the time. I think you are fabulous."

"Well, well! All these compliments on a Monday morning!" Kathryn cries as Irina smiles at their extravagance. "You'll turn Irina's head, Sheila."

"Thank you, darling"—Irina laughs—"but it will take more than compliments to turn my head. Still, you're very sweet, Sheila. Now go on, the two of you. You're probably full of secrets, like I was when I was a girl. So many secrets, so many dreams!" She sighs. "You too, Kathryn, I'll bet."

"Of course, of course," Kathryn says, and winks at Monica. "It's all right, go ahead, I'm going to stay here with your mother for a while."

Monica takes a pail and a rake, which they will need for the clamming.

"I'm going to take you to a marvelous place," Monica promises as she and Sheila walk along the road.

"Where?"

"You'll see when we get there."

"What were you going to tell me about myself that was so marvelous? I've been wondering and wondering."

"Can't tell you until we get there. How do you like Kathryn?"

"I *love* her. I wish I could stay with her forever and never go home. If I lived on this island, I would never leave."

Another Island lover; Monica sighs. But she is delighted to see Sheila open up, as it were. Is it the Island, actually, or Kathryn, or more simply being away from home and from school? Whatever it is, Monica finds, amazingly enough, that she likes Sheila more now than ever before.

"Tell me, Sheila, did you have a hard time getting here? I mean your folks actually *let* you come? Were they willing?"

"Are you serious? They were *furious*. There was a thing at church I was supposed to go to, but I told them you invited me . . . and you did, a long time ago. My mother wept and said I was disrespectful and my father said, 'There, look at what you're doing to your mother.' But Monica, you're the only friend I have and I had to see you, so I said some things."

"What things?"

"Like I would set myself on fire if I didn't go, although I wouldn't really do that, or I'd run away and if they locked me up I'd call the police 'cause they'd have to let me out sometime. Anyway, it scared them, I think, because in the end my father gave me some money but insisted I take the ferry back this afternoon, and so I promised him I would."

"But you stuck up for your rights! Sheila, I'm proud of you."

Monica is also proud that Sheila has told her parents that Monica is her best friend, but she feels guilty, because up to now Sheila has been more of a burden than anything else. But she will make up for it! As the thin watery roommate walks beside her with a hint of courage in her stride, Monica feels the stirrings of hope for her.

They have come to a point of land where a natural line of rocks stretches out to sea. Above it is the cliff where Monica lay on Sunday afternoon, looking down on these very rocks.

"We'll have to wait for the tide to go out," she says, settling on a rock. The air is brisk but the sun is warming. Shore birds run along the beach on thin stick legs. A flock of cormorants skim over the water.

"Now tell me," Sheila begs, "what is it you were going to tell me?"

"You just told *me*," Monica says. "You found out all by yourself."

"Found out what? What are you talking about?"

"You did something you wanted to do, for the first time in your life, I bet, and you wouldn't let your parents stop you. You were being *Sheila* and not some rag doll tossed here and there. It felt great, didn't it?"

"Yes, but what did you want to *tell* me?" Sheila could be brighter, Monica believes, and perhaps she will be when she is able to see more clearly.

"Only this—that you have to think things through for yourself and then do what you think is right. Of course you have to be responsible and you have to learn to lay ghosts to rest when the time comes."

"Monica, you're talking in circles. Ghosts?"

"Ghosts are ideas that were valid once but no more; if you hang on to them, they can strangle you. So let them go, open your hand like this and blow them away . . . phhhhhh!"

"Monica, you're really weird."

"No, love. Let me tell you about Crazy Hattie, a recluse on the Island. Her husband ran off with another woman and left her once, and nobody denies this was probably unfair. But if she'd had any sense she would have picked herself up, muttered the devil with them both, and done something else with her life. Instead she couldn't let go, so she let this affair strangle her and haunt her all her life, and it's turned her into a bitter old woman. That's extreme, of course, but everyone has ghosts." Even me, she thinks, but she has let her father go and now she will recover.

"Gee, Monica, I don't think I have any ghosts."

"Don't you? Think hard, Sheila."

"Nothing's ever happened to me. There was my brother, of course."

"And what about him?"

Sheila does not answer but kicks her foot against a stone as she gazes out to sea.

"Did you like your brother?"

Sheila bites her thumbnail, then turns suddenly to Monica. "I hated him. I never could tell anyone that, of course, and you won't tell anyone, will you?"

"Of course not."

"He's dead and I shouldn't say anything bad about the dead. But he was so perfect, so goddamn perfect—there, I said it—that the more perfect he was, the smaller I seemed to be. He called me The Twirp. That's all he ever called me. But I shouldn't say these things; he's dead."

"You can say what you want."

"My brother didn't like me, but he's gone. My parents keep talking about him and they don't really forgive me for not being him. They don't like me. The girls at school don't either. I wish I could go away, get out of it all . . ."

"I like you, Sheila. Really, it's true. I do. Maybe there's something you could try this summer. Something entirely new, like . . ."

She strains to think of something. The thought exists somewhere, vibrating in the air. It flies to her magically.

"*Doing*, Sheila, doing. You've always been sheltered, taught, raised, educated, and for the first time last week you *did* what you wanted. Now maybe you can think of doing something for someone else, giving something of yourself . . . it would be a good start."

"But I can't do anything. What can I *do*?"

"That's your decision. For a start you might offer to work in a Neighborhood House, or a Well-Baby Clinic, or do something with kids—take them on hikes, picnics, or teach them to read; there're lots of kids with reading problems. It's not as if you'd have to do it forever, but you would be *doing* something, which is a lot different from having something *done* to you or for you, you understand?"

"I never thought of it. I'm sort of afraid."

"Who isn't afraid, really? You could begin in a quiet way, with kids. Or maybe you could help out in the conversation classes for immigrants who need practice speaking English. I mean, it's not just that you're going to be a Lady Bountiful. People really need help. But they will give you something that you need too, like knowing that the world is bigger than your home and school. Besides, it would get you out of the house this summer."

"It's sort of scary, though. It's not easy for me to meet people. And what would my folks think?"

Monica laughs. "If you can tell them that you're going to the Island and you come here just like that, then you can say you're going to the Neighborhood House or whatever and simply do it. Don't worry about meeting people; you'll get used to it."

"Well, maybe. Oh Monica, I've never thought like this before. It's almost too much. Will you help me find a place?"

"Sure," Monica promises.

They sit quietly. Monica picks up a shell, perfect in its miniscule beauty, and hands it to Sheila, who thanks her, but approaches another subject hesitantly. "About yesterday morning, Monica. That was weird, if you want to know, your father and that whole bunch, all of them so tense or whatever. You aren't going back to Berkeley with your father, are you?"

"No, I guess not."

"I'm so relieved," Sheila cries, the words rushing out of her. "I was afraid that you'd leave, afraid for myself, but when I saw everyone, I was sort of afraid for you. It could be creepy. Do you feel bad about it, Monica?"

"Well. It wasn't easy, not any of it. But it's over. And I guess it's not a tragedy, because here we are, aren't we, the both of us. Look, I think the tide's out enough now so we can get some clams. Okay?"

They take off their shoes and socks, roll up their pants legs, and leap over the rocks to the shore. The sun blesses them as they dig for their dinner.

2

Irina

Kathryn drives Monica and Sheila to the dock in time for the two o'clock ferry. Sheila is radiant even though her sandy hair is askew and Irina's wildly striped sweater overwhelms the severity of the school uniform. She puts down her canvas luggage and the pasteboard box of clams she is taking to her parents and throws her arms first around Kathryn and then around Monica.

"Wow, I've never done that before. I hope it was all right," she apologizes.

"It was perfect!" Kathryn assures her, and Monica promises to see her on Wednesday night when she returns to school.

"This was the best time in my whole life," Sheila says; then she turns to walk up the ramp to *The Genessee Queen.*

"Kathryn, thanks so much for taking her. I've never seen her so nearly happy. It was the best thing that could have happened."

"Well, Monica, if I don't go to the mainland or the Outside World, whatever you call it, then I must expect it to come to me now and then."

"I don't expect she'll stay high like this. She gets depressed. But it was marvelous for her. She needed you and this weekend," Monica says.

"You can be very perceptive, you know," Kathryn says as she pulls up near Bittersweet Place. "But let's hear about *your* weekend."

"It bombed. One big explosion. Boom. And it's over."

"Monica, my dear, it can't be that easy for you."

"I'll recover. It's Irina I worry about. Did you notice how much older she seemed this morning?"

"It's only to be expected. People are always changing, looking older one minute, younger the next. Irina is very young, you know."

"Kathryn, she's thirty-five!"

"Tsk-tsk! And you think that's ancient, I suppose?" Kathryn winks at Monica, who is embarrassed, because Kathryn is probably close to thirty-five twice over. "Monica, your mother is beautiful, unique, and highly intelligent."

"Are you sure about the 'intelligent' part?"

"Yes. She is very wise."

"But she fails at everything. Look at her life, Kathryn, one failure after another. The only thing she hasn't failed at is what my father couldn't do. My mother loves us, has always loved us."

"You too are becoming wise."

"But I don't feel the least bit wise, Kathryn. I've got to help her, I know, but what can I do?"

"Play it by ear. You'll know when the time comes, just as you did with Sheila, I suspect."

"Kathryn, you are so good, so good, *so good*!"

"Here, here, Monica. This morning I ruined two perfectly good pots and the stream of profanity I let out doesn't quite qualify for your generous 'so good'! Now, if you'll come to my house for just a minute, I have a little gift for you."

She drives to her cottage, runs in, comes out again with a small porcelain statue—a tiny bird whose feathers are beaten back in the wind, yet he stands with his mouth open, shouting at the universe.

"Oh, oh, what a dear! I love him. Kathryn . . . you are so good to me. He's so tiny, yet so brave and strong."

"That's the message," Kathryn says, "and now it's time for you to scoot on home and see what your mother is up to."

Irina sits at the kitchen table and sips a cup of strong tea. She is very pale, her eyes are dark and tragic; her voice has dropped nearly an octave.

"Hello, Monica. Welcome to the soap opera."

"What do you mean?"

"It simply can't be believed. Here, read this letter. It just came."

Monica takes the typewritten sheet of paper.

Dear Irina:

I'm afraid our news may not be very comforting, but it seems as though we must put Bittersweet Place up for sale. We have been so glad to have you as a tenant; you've been terrific. But our taxes have gone up again and those necessary repairs you wrote to us about are costly beyond belief. So we have little choice in the matter but to sell.

We've been in touch with a real-estate agent and he thinks he has a buyer. Of course we'll insist on your being given fair notice. We're ever so sorry, but it seems the best thing to do under the circumstances.

With best wishes to you and the girls,
Don and Mary Canfield

"Well, so we're getting shoved out of the nest at last!" Monica remarks.

"Right!" Irina is close to tears. "This is such an awful weekend for you, Monica. I wish it were different."

"It's not all that bad," Monica says, although she believes it couldn't be much worse. "The air is clearing, at any rate. Only it's not very clear here. Mom, I wish you would stop smoking. Listen, let's take a walk in the sun. You've been in all day long."

"A walk, well . . . if that's what you want," Irina says. Never has she seemed more discouraged. Monica wouldn't have thought it possible.

"You're up to it, aren't you?" she asks gently.

"I can walk, if that's what you mean. I'm not exactly falling over because I'm such an old crock," Irina says. There, she is her vinegary old self, not entirely pleasant, but better than the forlorn Irina. "Where do you want to go?"

"Mount Albert."

"Way up there?"

"Mother, you can see out forever from there."

At any other time, Irina would have argued her out of it, because it is part of her nature to do so, but now she gives in, puts on a sweater and slaps a straw sun hat on her head. They say very little as they walk uphill, for they are both slightly breathless, yet Irina remarks:

"It's funny that we haven't gone walking for such a long time. When you were little, we went everywhere together. Do you remember Rome? What a city! Do you remember all those other places, those shops where we used to try on all kinds of clothes? It was naughty because we couldn't afford them, but who cares! It was fun. I loved having you with me."

"And I love being with you now," Monica says. She is pricked with guilt, however, for in making notes for her autobiography it was always her father she remembered, almost never her mother. Now she recalls vaguely trotting along beside her mother; she was such a very little girl then.

"There, you didn't think I could do it, did you?" Irina says breathlessly as they reach the top of the mountain and collapse under the pines. Then they walk to the edge where Monica sat alone the day before.

"It's such a magnificent island!" Irina says sadly.

"Yup. But we've had it, Mom. They're kicking us out. The signs are all around. Anyway, there's no reason for us to stay now."

"Oh no?" Irina and Monica have barely discussed Josef, and it is still a touchy subject for Irina.

"We came here so that someday he would come for us. Well, he's come and gone. Harsh but true. The funny part is, I almost feel sorry for that little pianist living with him, or at least I'd be sorry if I liked her. I never knew how vain Daddy is."

"And I'd forgotten," Irina says. "Even so . . ."

"Mother, he's very smooth in an old-fashioned way and he's a good violinist, he really is, but in other ways he can be awfully boring."

"Monica, he's your father!"

"Which doesn't mean he isn't someone who always has to play his little games. I almost think we're lucky that he didn't take us back."

"Why, Monica!" Irina says, shocked, and then she begins to laugh, a painful laugh that is close to tears. "I hate to confess it, but the same thought occurred to me. I guess things have changed."

"When do we leave the Island?"

"What do you mean, 'leave the Island'? Why, I love it here."

"That's not what you told Josef."

"You're right. Well, I love it and I hate it. It's all confused. With Josef coming and going, I can't think straight. I feel hollowed out, as if someone had plucked out my very center."

"That's not your center, Mom. Not Josef. He was just an illusion after all this time. Look, Mama, let's go away, all three of us, to someplace we've never been. Gabrielle can take ballet lessons at an academy, and she should—Mother, she's terrific. We can't let her grow into another Island child. You didn't let it happen to me."

"I guess I didn't think about it. I always thought we'd go back to Berkeley with your father. Good heavens, what an idiot I am!"

"No, Mother, not that. You tried something and it didn't work."

"My dear child, I have tried hundreds of things and each one has been a failure."

"Then we'll have to think of something you haven't tried. It might just work."

"What might just work?"

"Something entirely new. Kathryn has a friend who wants to train a travel agent. In Seattle. Kathryn thinks you'd be perfect."

"Me? Monica, I don't know if I could do it."

"Why not? You've been everywhere. You were the one who used to make all the arrangements when we went on tours with Daddy. Anyway, when you talk about a place, you make people think they have to go there, it must be so marvelous."

"Yes, Monica? You think so? You know that for a fact?" She hugs her, rocks back and forth with her affectionately. "Well, I'm not so sure. I've been on this island so long, I don't know how I can leave it."

"Sure you do. You told me when we first came here. *The Genessee Queen*, the faithful queen, that comes here every day, rain or shine, will take us back to the mainland or the Mainstream or the Real World."

"All we have to do is pack and go, I suppose."

"I think so, Irina."

"What a dreamer you are! Well, I don't know. I'll think about it tomorrow. Okay?"

The afternoon sun is beginning to sink, sending out long shadows across the fields below. Irina stands up and stretches. "It was nice living here, wasn't it, Monica?"

Monica nods in agreement and the two of them walk down the mountain.

The Last Chore

That evening after a brief dinner, Monica clears the kitchen table and then sits there with type-writer, pencils, and a pile of snowy paper. Gabrielle leans on her elbows at an impossible angle from the kitchen table and looks up into her sister's face. "Whatcha doin'?"

"Writing. And I need quiet and patience and understanding and love and none of your tricks, Gaby. I've got to get this paper done before Wednesday night, and I haven't even begun!"

"How long does it have to be? What's it about?" Gabrielle asks.

"I don't know. I'll begin at the beginning and end at the end, or at least where everything seems to be right now. It's the story of my life."

"Weird. Monica, will you put me in it, huh?"

"Sure, if you're good. I'll say wonderful things about you."

"Do you want me to tell you what I want you to say?"

Monica laughs. "You have to write your own script, sweetie. I can't do it for you and you can't do it for me. Too bad!"

"That's okay. I don't think I'll go over to Rosemary's tonight. I'd rather stay home with you."

"I'm glad, and now will you let me get started on this?"

Gabrielle skips to the other room and soon begins her new lesson on the piano. "Welcome, Sweet Springtime." And Monica settles down to write. A title announces itself in her mind and she writes it at the top of the page. THE END OF A CHILDHOOD. She pauses. The title suggests sadness, but not a tragedy. Childhood ends, one way or another.

And then she begins to write.